NAMBÉ
YEAR ONE

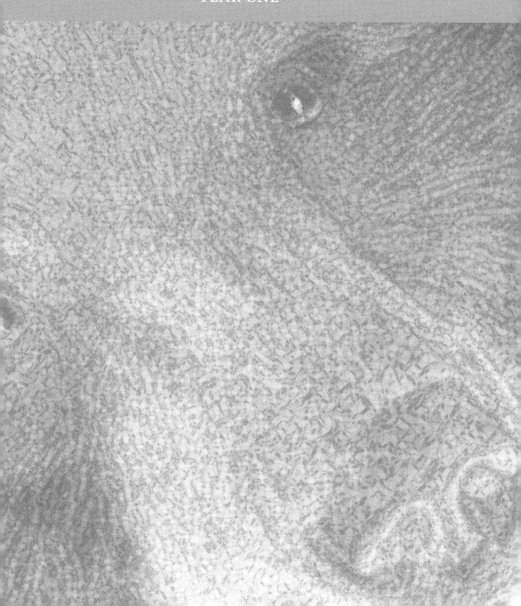

Having learnt early to suffer, we suffer not at all. . . .
[T]he cruelest torment does not make us tremble;
and we shrink from no form of death, which we have
learnt to scorn. When we see fit, we make no difference
between yes and no; well can we be martyrs,
but confessors never. . . . We sing loaded with
chains and in the deepest dungeons.
                    Cervantes—on the Gypsies—1614

A Gypsy woman nursed him;
that is why he has wings.
                    Serbian song

Nambé
year one

Orlando Romero

Foreword by Thomas E. Chávez

UNIVERSITY OF NEW MEXICO PRESS ◆ ALBUQUERQUE

University of New Mexico Press edition
   published 2009 by arrangement with the author.
Printed in the United States of America

14 13 12 11 10 09   1 2 3 4 5 6

LIBRARY OF CONGRESS CATALOGING-IN-PUBLICATION DATA
Romero, Orlando, 1945–
  Nambé—year one / Orlando Romero ;
  foreword by Thomas E. Chávez.
    p. cm.
  ISBN 978-0-8263-4632-2 (PBK. : ALK. PAPER)
1. Gypsies—Fiction. 2. New Mexico—Fiction.
I. Title.
  PS3568.O5645N3 2009
  813'.54—dc22

                2008037856

Book design and type composition by Kathleen
  Sparkes
Book is composed using Warnock Pro OTF 11.5/15, 26P.
  Display type and ornaments are also Warnock Pro.

A la hembra, puerta de los

misterios del universo.

FOREWORD

An intellectual knowledgeable about Hispanic New Mexican literature once told me that Orlando Romero had to be included as one of New Mexico's most important literary figures if, for nothing else, because of his novel *Nambé Year One*. The book, he continued, stood alone as a classic of New Mexican literature.

At the time of that conversation the novel had been out of print for many years. A whole generation and more had no easy access to the book nor had they the opportunity to delve into its invaluable insights into northern New Mexico people and their world views that are pertinent to all of humanity. The University of New Mexico Press has corrected this gross oversight so that many more serious readers and students of literature will be intellectually challenged as they ponder Romero's words and thoughts.

Nambé Year One is an act of genius that is all the more amazing considering the fact that the author created this novel with the apparent knowledge and wisdom of a man who had lived for centuries. Yet, he wrote this stand-alone tome as a young man.

Romero's book is a novel, but not just a novel. It is philosophy, a metaphysical self-exploration into faith, heritage, and humanity. It is autobiographical but more, for its points are universal. He writes about love and death. Love, in a sense beyond any standard definition, is a kind of spiritual organism. Death is not death but memory and a spiritual blood that literally carries on through future generations. Both love and death are symbolically seen in the stars and this celestial allusion is constant.

He poses the question, "What would happen . . . when all the old ones were gone? Who would counsel us and give us answers written on the petals of wild flowers?" His book contains the answer that is Romero's green-eyed gypsy, a personal spiritual being hidden within all of us to one degree or another. She personifies desire, fear, knowledge, empathy, a sense of reality, and a place in time that Romero is able to identify as a part of his own self. He also constantly reminds each individual, if he or she cares enough, to explore and then share their experience with others.

As may be gathered, this is a book about surface simplicity and subsurface complexity. We all accept ourselves superficially but rarely consider the otherness that makes us who we are. We make no attempt to understand or even acknowledge the historical and spiritual depths that really define our selves. Orlando Romero offers a road map to both with an in-depth attempt at comprehension and a clear acknowledgment of the lessons encountered.

Even the book's organization parallels the message, for, to use a popular analogy, it is truly a forest with many interesting trees, but the trees can distract the reader from the overall picture of a beautiful forest. The book is almost a series of essays, but not quite. It is sprinkled with short stories that may or may not be essays. But, without the whole, the stories have little meaning. The stories and essays, as they stand alone, refer to thoughts and concepts that make more sense in the overall story. Everything is interrelated.

As I read the book for the second time I began to comprehend that the message of this book is not for the self-centered and self-fooled, those people with pretensions of superiority. This is a book for the weak and lost who are really neither, for they are determined and strong enough to want to know the "why" and "what" of their very being. Thus the latter are superior and the former are permanently lost.

On a personal note, when I suffered a death in the family, Orlando Romero consoled me with allusions to shooting stars. I thought I understood. Now, with the second edition of *Nambé Year One* ready, I understand.

This work is a contribution that stands among the stars, for, truly, it is as valuable.

Thomas E. Chávez

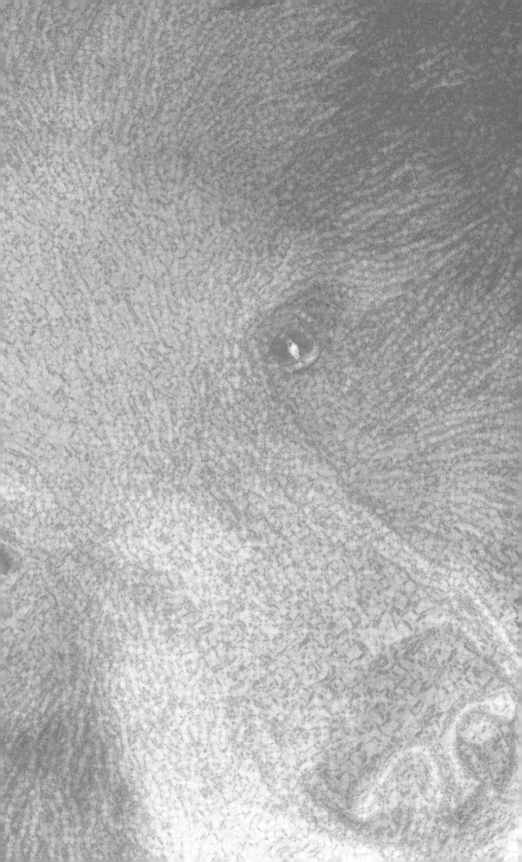

Nambé—Year One ≡

≡ In the time of the Gypsies and Payasos that wandered through the mountains of Northern New Mexico, there was one particular enchantress who came from Spain. Her companion was a magnificent dancing bear. She was beautiful and haunting beyond description, and it was said that with her green eyes she could capture the soul of any man. One look into her chambers of green magic and the magnetism of her eyes uprooted a man's soul and rendered it helpless as it burst through his breast.

Realizing her power, the Gypsy wore dark green-colored lenses in round, gold frames. Her eyes she could submerge, but she could not hide the aura of her gracefulness, of her face, body or soul. This brought on, like thundering daybreak, the stares of women and the wonder of men. In every village the experience was the same. Every man wanted to be touched and consumed by her. Where she walked she left the essence of lilacs, apricot blossoms, and herbal memories.

But every man knew that to touch her was to die. It was rumored that her dancing bear was an enchanted prince who would rip the flesh of any man who dared touch her. The bear, in his ponderous size and wild beauty, was as close to her as a lover.

These thoughts opened my eyes as I stared into the dark abyss beyond me. My wife's fluorescent body lay beside me and, as my restlessness increased on our bed, she turned to face me. The movement of my eyes and my soul staring into the darkness had awakened her. As she moved her dark sensuous body close to mine I could feel the glow from her garden.

Gently opening her eyes she saw my solitude. With her hand she touched my cheek and, kissing her palm, I ran my tongue along her lifelines. Her heat increased and half-asleep she held the ember that would light her flame. There was a cosmic fusion that threw my thoughts to wander from one constellation to another. My body quivered as the ligaments that held my muscles lost all control and I lay exhausted between two pastures where memories of childhood clung to green and growing life.

I lay relieved as I stared in the darkness at the adobe walls. I could hear the voices of children, my own voice among them, then the Gypsy's, and then my Mother's.

"Mateo, I've told you time after time to stop eating the earth of this wall. If you persist in showing Miguel your obsession, I will have to put a bit on you like your Grandfather's plowhorse."

She held tightly to a worn leather strap as she paused in her words, a pause that vibrated and cracked the wall that held back leaks of childish tears. Confidently she added, "This afternoon I'm going to ask your Grandfather to calcimine these walls."

Her previous efforts had proved futile. She had placed the hottest chili she could find—and eventually vinegar—on the adobe walls to stop my gnawing.

The darkness is in the center now, but there is a gray shadow surrounding it. Again children's voices echo in the caverns of my soul. A rivulet runs down its wall. The adobe earth, dampened by the sweet rain, is pulling me. Reaching for it, I take a rounded pebble of adobe that lay at the wall's foundation. Its aroma enters my mouth, shoves itself up my veins, rapes my thoughts and, in its essence, relieves me.

In that part of the soul, in this house and this place where time

Orlando Romero

means nothing and everything, relief means only fleeing shadows and images that glow in the dark—like joy—but which can also disappear like the joy of a burdened woman.

In this continuous restlessness the Gypsy entered my solitude again. In part, it was this house. It was my Great Grandfather's, my Grandfather's, my Father's, and now mine. Its walls are alive with the tears of years forgotten to the meaningless word we know as time. It was fact. This house kept hidden and forgotten secrets within its worn floorboards. Every step taken on them was recorded and memorized. And, like our childhood catechism, nothing was beyond belief. It caught time itself, made it stop, and its haunting memories were left as reminders. Other times as well as these were only echoes, vibrations and waves of energy that, as if by accident, had been thrown into the earth that went to make these walls as well as our physical and spiritual beings.

It had been my Grandfather's courtesy and love for the joyous and unusual that brought every traveling troupe to spend the night in this house. Attracted by her beauty and the transmission of feelings that crossed and bridged their loneliness and solitude, he asked the Gypsy and her bear to spend the night.

Today, my Grandfather sits with his elbows on the table and a gentle violin voice fills the purple of the room. A full head of silver gray and glowing golden brown skin with furrows only his plow could conceive are part of his image. His calm is an illusion. A wild, frantic gleam fills his eyes. His vision goes beyond my face and past these walls to a place where a road rips the stillness and turns the stagnancy of living into dream songs of wild joy and revelry, to an instant in energy that leaped his soul like the quaking beat and forwardness of the Taos drums, to a place beside the soul of the Gypsy with the dancing bear. My Grandfather has been touched by her aura, and his emanations are both confusing and profound as they enter his living blood in the cyclic pattern nature has deemed his grandson.

I am the incarnation of his wild blood, that hybrid solar-maize plant blood. There is Indian in us, of ancient forgotten peoples that roamed the world before there was history. I felt it the night I was seven years old.

We had the lamp under the salt cedar and the radiance of the moon reflected over the seven-acre field. Moonbeams as cool and clear as diamonds played on the water. From the light of the moon and the sun the maize would grow. At this moment, an owl was heard as if someone was directing a sensual symphony of crickets, frogs, and owls while the sweet smell of the earth in its virginity was once again being kissed by the water from the acequia. I knew it then. These were not shadows, but silhouettes, gigantic Easter Island heads that stared at us in our solitude, telling us that we were of the land, of these Sangre de Cristo Mountains with their violet-colored hues portraying the time when man is expelled from his mother's womb into the womb or earthen jar where all men find and reflect upon their primal essence—the energy of the universe, and the magnetism of the earth.

But this womb is my pleasure, the same pleasure that can disguise itself, or can turn into a prison. It was the same for my antepasados. Our salvation comes in knowing that every particle of life and energy comes from it. Our tragedy and our joy come from our sensitivity to it.

It was this sensitivity that reflected the similarities between our souls and the constant, elemental Gypsies who have been and who have left their images and souls to lie side by side with ours. The Gypsy that was my Grandfather's—or in him—is the Gypsy that is mine.

"She spent the night here with her bear beside her. They lay on the sheepskins I had by the stove in the kitchen. I went around to the kitchen window so that I could see her without her colored lenses."

My Grandfather lit his hand-rolled cigarette and the smoke whirled past the hawk of his nose.

"She didn't take her lenses off first. She untied the knot in the

Orlando Romero

scarf covering her breasts. I stood paralyzed while my young heart pounded. When she removed her long skirt, the bear gently put his arms around her. As she took off her lenses she glanced in the direction of the window. The kerosene lamp was dim and yellowish-brown. For a second, rays of golden and green particles filled the entire room as she lay concealed by the bear's enormous back."

His words of green, gold, and yellowish-brown tint the prism that surrounds me.

In my restlessness I imagine the hour, for in this house there are no clocks or other man-made devices that try to measure time. When I reach the kitchen, I don't need the light of electric lamps. I am his grandson and my way is lightened by the glow left in the walls by the Gypsy. Slicing an apple and some cheese, I open a bottle of Spanish wine.

The glow is there. It has been there every day and every night since her herbal essence and the blossoms of her soul touched mine. The glow has been there since I realized she was beyond any Dulcinea the poets could conceive.

It wasn't planned. Love, life, and death are never planned. I saw her in school one evening as she finished bathing her body and soul in the fountain of her magic. When she smiled at me, I knew composers had taken her burdened laughter; its notes had been their music. When she held my arm and lay the darkness of my hand against the gentleness of her face, I knew that we had crossed and fused into one wild leap through the moon.

I saw it. Her long, gentle hands gave away one of her secrets. They were an extension of her soul.

I must sleep. Tomorrow we have our turn at watering. Here in Nambé everything evolves in and around cycles. When I have completed my turn. I shall be buried under the apricot tree. My rot shall enrich its roots. But, tomorrow, I must water all the trees, the garden, and also the thirst of ancestral memories that go down one thousand feet below Nambé.

Irrigating—Part 1 ≡

≡ A smiling and confused face looks across the breakfast table. The eggs have been sprinkled with green chile. She turns and returns with a cup of black coffee for herself. I have tried to convince her that black coffee is bad for her stomach, but she persists, the way I persist in my smoking. The birds of yellow and green and the colors of early summer have entered and are feeding around our table.

"This morning you must bring me good soil before you start to irrigate. I want to place these flowers in larger pots."

She reflects with the warmth of the sun. "Look at them, aren't they beautiful?"

They were. When I first brought her to this house, she knew little of planting and growing things. Now after five measured years her beauty and grace were maturing like the flowers she had planted on the earth and in our children.

With the shovel in the back of my old truck I drove toward the Sangre de Cristo Mountains. To reach the ditch where I was to separate and rechannel the water into the ditch that we use, I had to walk a quarter-mile from the truck. There is green at the edges of the ditch. There is an intense blue above me as a hawk swoops down fifty yards from me and I hear the painful scream of life entering another form.

It runs smooth. The magnetism of Nambé pulls the water up a steep grade and then down again. It sings as it consumes crickets, ants and other creatures that are crossing its path. In the early spring we had cleaned its banks and scraped its bottom. There are dry callouses on my hands from the spring ritual. The ritual is as necessary as planting seed and breathing.

Today, just like today. I was thirteen or so in measured years and time, and I liked them all. But there was one special rubia, part Indian and part Irish. And everywhere the young strong voices of old men sang "Las Mañanitas." The songs I learned in the church choir were there. The Feast of Corpus Christi, with the handmade altars surrounded by wild flowers and the yellow, orange, and white petals that were thrown in the path of the girl chosen to play the Virgin, this followed and colored all my visions.

She was my first. This is the way time is measured here. In seasons, love, joy and pain. So that all joy is the same, only stronger. Pain matters, but here it allows the soul the ability to take more. Death is not dying, but coming back again to nourish living things.

I have not seen her since, but images remain to sweeten my life. Her image is dimmer though, since the Gypsy entered my solitude. Everywhere, like the white foam at the edge of the ditch that needs the current to move, the same energy transmits my Grandfather's voice and his words about the Gypsy with the dancing bear.

"Next morning, when I awoke from a dream, she asked to read my palm. Thinking about the bear and his ferocity, I almost said no. With her gentle gestures she reached for my hand and I sat there in amazement as the bear stood around us without a trace of danger."

My Grandfather's voice got heavier in the white foam of my memory.

"His shadow around us seemed to darken the room. He stood there like a symbol of infertile fertility. Were they lovers? Was the bear a reflection of herself, or the secret she carried deep in her soul? As she read my palm and smoothly caressed my lifelines, she said I was to marry a dark woman who was not my lover. Then she paused and the glow of her face dimmed the white of the walls, turning it to gray and shadows of cooling blue. She continued by saying I would never have to work for anyone else but myself, and that I was to live in health through my old age. When she looked through my palm, she said that even though I would marry, I was to live alone."

As I left the ditch to run for itself and find its way home, I kept thinking that my Grandfather's Gypsy had been right. My Grandmother died at an early age. I never knew her physically. And my Grandfather never remarried.

He worked his hands at a flour mill, and its reputation soon brought Indian farmers from Cochiti to Taos. My brightest memories come from helping him in that mill. In the resolana, the Indians and their primeval language and manners filled the early autumn air with the link that bound all of us in the circle that were our neighboring valleys. Yet they were a level above me, pulling me toward them. They were surrounded by the color orange, as if a tiger and a woman lay in their breasts.

Irrigating—Part 2

Sitting on the ground like my ancestors, I can watch the water as it quenches little maize plants. I water only four furrows at a time and with just enough water so that it appears to creep and dissolve into the soil. There are tractors in Nambé but my Grandfather and I have chosen to plow with a horse and to plant by hand. There is no need in going deep and disturbing our bones.

I have planted maize since the early springs of my life. For every plant that breaks the surface there is in me one hundred years of joy. From the maize plant we have secured the nourishment of our physical spirit by eating and drinking it in countless forms. Unlike the foreigner Coffee, El Atole, which is made of blue cornmeal, calms and with its substance fortifies the body against the evil spirits of sickness.

My friends at college tell me that I am fortunate to own such fine land, good animals, and generations of history which they believe comes from "joyous, melancholy Spain." In their eyes I am colorful, charming, romantic, even picturesque. But few have seen, even fewer have known me. Only that one burdened soul has touched me.

In cycles I become depressed at this college. There are few instructors that stimulate me. My years have been measured at twenty-seven though my soul is older than the world and as young and joyous as my love for the Gypsy. Yet had it not been for school, her aura would have eluded me—but only briefly.

We are destined to meet one another. Lovers, brothers and sisters, sons and fathers. Though there may be no physical brother or mother or lover, our souls search to meet what is to be shared. We shared each other's burden and joy and it soared like a wild bird. Not to be consumed by the heat of love or the sun, but by the mother that is the garden. By accident or by nature, we all carry in our souls the fertility of the earth and the mother.

She knew it; we both knew it. She ran to me and away from me because in her soul not only was there passion but also the burden and echoes of a time when the word "man" meant something else. Yes, quite vividly I hold in a part of my soul and memory the seed which reflects yesterday's todays as bright, stunning, mellow and gentle scenes. She lumbers forward like a boy, an adolescent, knowing that the whole world is a special place because he is discovering the sweetness and the potency of his sensuality. Only she and I share this special secret.

I shared it the day she placed the softness of her hand against the darkness of mine. It was too late. From that very instant we were bound and chained to each other. It was a golden chain that didn't tie us to earthly bounds and limitations but which transformed our feet to wings. We kicked our heels to the moon one night; I showed her how. And while the moon was bright and warm on a cold winter night, she flung herself forward under her cape in imitation of her favorite Payaso. She laughed and then we both laughed. Our echoes penetrated the cracks of all those lonely lost souls whose only joys exist in the resurrection of pleasant memories, forgotten memories that break the stagnancy of depression.

And then from deep inside of her, where humans always lock

Orlando Romero

secrets, her melancholy surfaced. It reflected in my eyes and in the Sangre de Cristo Mountains that trap our joy. She knew it from my eyes; I understood her in her deepest dungeon. The joy of her soul is tremendous, the sorrow profound.

In our bond of sharing and exchanging, though at times not consciously aware of it, we came to understand the heaviness of each other's burden. Because of this, she became my calm.

———

My friend the scholar says that the name Romero means going to Rome. I don't believe we've found Rome or ever will find it. The Moor, the Jew, the Arab, Spanish and Indian blood force us to live by the law of nature and its mystical powers in the valleys of the Sangre de Cristos, not by the laws made in the minds of men. We balance precariously on the peaks of the land and, distracted by the Gypsies, our physical and spiritual lives are prolonged and sensualized by our acceptance of them.

———

The water has darkened all the rows where seed is planted; the irrigating is almost complete though there is never enough water to quench this soil.

As I lean my head against the twenty-foot-high shoulder of the pond, my eyes clearly perceive colors of yellow and black. A timeless second later, the perception seems hazy. My mind cannot grasp. In the midafternoon sun, there is enough clear light except for an obscurity encircling a Salamander's head. Frogs, toads, snakes, snails and Salamanders occasionally bask on the pond's shoulder, but this is more than a Salamander. The haze decreases and reverses itself so that now it is around the sun and the earth. The only clear vision that I can comprehend is centered on the pond and the Salamander.

His head is enormous. It doesn't seem possible that this creature is twenty times the size of the six-inch Salamanders that live here. He is almost godlike in his awesomeness. Instantly, as he mentions my name, a blast of frozen air hits me as a solid force.

"Come here, Mateo Romero! Look around you that the fire in your soul is about to consume you."

As if pulled by a trance, I follow his order to come up to him at the bank of the pond.

"Mateo, you have a choice in this matter."

I felt only nausea. As children we were warned never to swim naked in the pond. We were told that Salamanders sought our posteriors to make their homes. But following his directions, I balanced myself up to the edge of the bank and we both gazed at the far side of the pond. On a scar I had never noticed before sat the Gypsy of my universe, her presence softening and settling the air. Her long skirt reflected the invisible sun in the golden scales that covered it. The illusion that appeared before me revealed the hair, face and breasts as hers, the rest an underwater goddess.

The Salamander turned his entire being. In a leap I found myself a few feet above the ground as his six-foot tail almost knocked me down. As he returned his look to my eyes, his refrigerated breath once again chilled me.

"I have been summoned by the Earth gods to quench the fire that would remove you from your ancestral bones. With one breath, mortal, I can surround your Gypsy in a prison of watery ice. It is the desire of your soul that will determine her fate, as well as yours."

$$\Longrightarrow\Longleftarrow$$

The sun turns bright again but I have trouble rising. Extremely dizzy, I make my way down to the bottom of the bank where I have left my hoe. It must have been the heat. My Grandfather's words echo.

"La gente de antes kept Salamanders close to their homes in case of fire. Surrounding a fire, Salamanders would quickly extinguish the hottest flame."

Orlando Romero

These were our people, the people who are buried one thousand feet below Nambé.

The sun will be setting soon. Once again the color of Christ's passion will envelope the valley, all valleys, because this is the place that experienced the beginning.

From shades of wine, purple, lavender, magenta, the mountains will capture the dying sun. Their fluorescent glow will color the image, or the illusion that seemed the reality, at the far side of the pond. The Gypsy will be returned to the color of her womb.

Studying ≡—

≡ Sitting with a bottle of Mexican beer and surrounded by books on the wall, I leaf and prepare for examinations tomorrow. Tomorrow, also, there is the possibility that I shall see her again. My life has been powered by the possibilities that weave dreams into images of reality. I awake fully on the second crow of the jet-black cock's command, realizing that today presents a new possibility to create, to form, and to shape the illusions of my highest ideal, even though I know that everything created must perish.

But it was in believing the possible that a night, two or three years ago in measured time, confirmed my world of possibilities. It must have been three or four in the morning, my hands incapable of closing my fingers or holding a carving tool any longer, when I looked with a weary yet joyous soul at my work. The exhaustion was produced by the frenzy of hands creating lines on wood, flowing with energy drained from the cosmos where my soul had collided with the Master of northern New Mexico woodcarvers. I felt the depths of his sorrow and the heights of his joy. Every carved line went beyond the human form to lines coming directly from the soul, bypassing the mind. The power was such that my hands could not control it.

There, sitting all alone in the world, I knew I had received some of the power and magic that was in the Mastercarver of New Mexico. From that fleeting and agonizing moment I was no longer satisfied with carving Santos. I had to go beyond my own experience, into all cultures, all religions, creatures and men.

So is it with the burden and the joy that is in me. I have constantly gone beyond the living and the physical, into a world my Gypsy once believed to exist only in my mind. But sometimes this same magic or power frightens me. Having completed these travels, a total sense of aloneness sets in.

"Grandfather," I asked in my memory, when the sun was stunning and the air so brittle and still that I thought my voice and words would destroy the niche we knew as Nambé.

"What did the Gypsy do after she read your palm?"

In the shade of the apricot tree in spring bloom, the whiteness of the blossoms surround his face.

"I was left confused and pensive. A lonely life I had not envisioned. But then, that is not what she said. She said I was to live alone. Today, reflecting on yesterday and tomorrow, I have lived alone. But I have done this only in the sense that I have not always been in physical contact with a woman. In the deepest memories of my being, I have never lived alone."

The air in its shattering heaviness seemed suffocating, and the sun seemed as if a suspended orange had taken its place. He paused in his words.

"But," I questioned, "what became of the Gypsy?" I searched further into a realm of which I knew I was a part.

With the stillness being broken by the cawing of crows, as if they were foretelling clouds and rain in our lives, my Grandfather's young lips emitted memories that lay beyond the bark of the apricot tree, not going to its roots but reaching and unflinchingly ignoring the brightness, reaching up beyond all earthly ties.

"I had to follow her. There was nothing else I could do. The restlessness in me tore me from this place as if it meant nothing because there was nothing like the gravity of her soul. There was no reasoning, only the tensions of my spirit as it was flung up to the high passes of Tres Ritos in search of her. I searched for months, asking, questioning, begging, hopelessly reaching out for answers that were not there.

"She hadn't stopped anywhere, knowing she had the power to change. On the last day, reaching the highest pass, I met a wagon. Its people told me of terrible bear moans, shouts and crying that they heard as they made a turn on the trail!"

On his face there was a weight unknown to me. His eyes dimmed and the golden furrows on his face became gray, distant shadows. The heat of Nambé lost its intensity, and crows covered the sky.

"Look," he said, pointing to the crows.

"They know what happened. I found her earrings among pieces of shredded clothing. The area was covered with blood and its heat returned to my nostrils as sweet. I should have been terrified and my soul full of a tremendous sense of loss. But, instead, the place and its canyons echoed with a serene calm. To this day I do not know who or what was consumed or devoured there. Neither the Gypsy nor the Bear were to be seen again. Only a haunting, melodic, and lost cry of a babe could be heard. That babe was your Father. In that instant, we were the only living creatures who had witnessed the disappearance of the Gypsy with the dancing bear."

My memory, mind, and soul, are rampant. Like three white horses all the same, like the Trinity carved by the old Santeros, there seems to be no difference. The end will be like the beginning. In my lifetime life forces come in threes.

I must study for my examinations tomorrow. I leaf through

Goethe, but I look at my carving tools and I want to carve. Then echoes from the adobe walls stare and minutely pick at the memory of my Father. In this house there is no escape.

≡≡

"Mateo, be quiet. You will scare them."

Then only greenness. Then water. So cold and clear that the bottom of the beaver pond is as visible as the candy store-front memories of childhood. Cautiously I pick up my boots and gently place them so the wild cutthroat trout will not feel my presence.

Here, among the tall pines, with a bottle of cheap wine in his pocket and flyrod in his hand, is forged one of the most enduring memories of my childhood. The water spiders frantically skim the surface. A beaver holds his stance for a moment and disappears into his background. There is no other image of my Father that will remain so pleasantly clear in my memory. He is himself, here in the woods. The cheap wine need not be in his back pocket. Only the wild in its beauty will make him forget it.

Together on our knees, he cautiously moves the flyrod slightly over his shoulder. The whip of the line gently places a tiny man-made fly on the water's surface. In a brilliant spray of clear water tinted like the prism of a rainbow, the wild cutthroat trout has been deceived. A struggle ensues and three wild leaps follow. Exhausted, the struggle has proved futile for the trout.

"Look at her, Mateo. She's beautiful."

In the clarity of the mountain air the trout is golden, and the wild, red slashes at its throat are more beautiful than a crown of red rubies.

My Father's hands gently release her and his voice will echo in me until the instant my eyes can no longer see the weeping in men's souls.

"No, my wild beauty, you are too magnificent to keep!"

He paused and tears were only visible to me because I knew

what he meant. He reached and felt the ugly contours of the pain-killer he held in his back pocket, but the weight of the willow fork with six or seven trout on it changed his mind.

This image was the reason I returned from my hiding. Centuries later, at age twelve or so, I hit him with a piece of firewood as he was about to beat my Mother. Two weeks were spent in the woods, hiding, sleeping, crying, dreaming, and longing for the warmth of my Mother's arms, the smiles, and my Brother's and Sister's laughter, and the mildly righteous wisdom of my Grandfather's words.

There in the woods, on a dark opal night, I saw it for the first time. A laughing, weeping, mocking star stared at me and witnessed my fate as a believer. Cold and warm, she looked down and through me. This was one of my first reflections on possibility. I would never again close myself from the possibility that all men need love, compassion, understanding, peace, kindness, and a chance for the soul to express itself. She saw the physical tears, but in my depths she saw the joy. I laughed deep inside because my misery was so insignificant compared to the rest of humanity. Quickly, I returned home.

Tonight, here with my studies, the first days of May are as puzzling as the doubts that surround me and my concern over examinations tomorrow. The May day's heat is followed by cold, chilling breezes. All day I've heard my children's voices. Sometimes they cry, but they play well together and are constant friends and companions. My geese wobble like comedians when they strike at anything that does not meet their approval. The perversity of their nature surfaces. But are they perverse, or are they the reflection of this strange May? Here in Nambé I've never known a cold or windy May. My maize plants bend like palm trees and the three newborn black kittens hold and embrace each other.

Three white horses, the Trinity, the Gypsy and her two elusive loves, my wife and two children, my Grandfather and his two worlds. I am surrounded by the life force of three.

Orlando Romero

My white cat with one blue and one green eye, born totally deaf, gave birth to three black kittens. Their father sits outside on the window sill, looking intently at my pretense at studying.

Many times I have wished I was a cat living high in the Sangre de Cristos. Wild and free, silky and swift, I would wait and wait, watching over my domain. Then slowly she would ride her horse by my lair. With one wild leap and cry I would pounce on her and rip her soul from its physical niche. Running swiftly, holding her heart in my jaws, I would take it to my cave.

Now it is mine and guarded by my murderous love, flourished by the vigil of my love, her Gypsy body would spiritually reappear and grow into mine.

Ancestral Ghosts

and Serpents ═══

═══ For two months now an eagle has been following me. The first time I saw him in his wild beauty and military splendor, the rising sun shone like the first orange apricot of the season as his mighty wings expanded in a power dive.

The rugged Bandelier Canyon vibrates with his cry. The giant walls of the canyon, sharp and ravaged by time and the elements, destroy the twentieth century. I am constantly awaiting attack by a brutal prehistoric creature. This is the canyon where my people walk in their sleep. Sharp stones, the smell of sagebrush, tall pines and the Rio Grande running high and turbulent remind me that part of my soul lay in this seemingly foreign place.

I had seen hundreds of caves in this canyon, but in the mirrors of my memory I instantly knew that my ancestral bones below Nambé were the same as these before me.

Two steps away, a rattlesnake warns me. This is the land of Serpents and Ghosts. Ghosts of Indians in their caves, children playing and crying. Old, ancient people dying, being reborn in the blackness and stillness of cave society, as the great, primal essence is absorbed. The paintings in the caves remain as proof of man's mystery, love, and involvement in the sometimes bewildering events in nature. Here, man has taken a bit of himself and painted his fancy, fantasy, and his reality.

On a high limb of a decaying pine, the talons cling. Is he following me? Whose flesh will they rip? Whose soul will be transformed when their sharpness invades, like an army, the physical creature that exists in a domain where it is natural for one species to live from another's death?

When the Gypsy and I were together, I wondered who would devour who. Was it natural to us that one soul should live and feed on another? Or were we to transcend our natural bonds to a place where love meant the mutual joy and suffering of our souls?

In laughter, joy and song, the Gypsy twirls and the eagle disappears. The violin haunts and the tambourines eroticize in staccato beats. Endless jumping, licking campfire flames kiss her breasts and part her legs as the passion for my Gypsy is renewed. Our heat is of a finer color, more orange than red. Because our secret is unique and our souls have touched each other, our heat has gone beyond this world.

Behind me the Bandelier Canyon is only a shadow. Thinking of the Gypsy's green eyes as clear mountain pools, I run to the Tres Ritos Stream. Here I find quiet comfort and solitude for the restlessness and turbulence in my soul.

There is an invader in this stream. He devours the young of the rainbow and cutthroat trout. He was brought here in the 1800s, but is considered by many as a native.

In the intensity and clearness of the suffocating blue sky, the tall pines and the stream's gurgle, my Father's lonely desolate voice echoes from an empty bottle of wine that has been discarded by the stream. "Por estar encantados con la vida, nuestras lágrimas nunca pararán. I am tossed about, in and out, vomited and excreted by serpents and creatures that have faces like men. Smiling, cold and cruel, their snake-like tongues lick away at the foundation of my essence. They place their seed of lust, jealousy, murder and violence in the wounds they have licked open. From these seeds sprout other cruel beings who begin wars over again among themselves. And there is biting, thunder, gunsmoke, fire and bottomless pits that keep pulling me further and further into the depths where my anguished cry for relief is as faint as the flutter of the Gypsy Moth's wings.

Sometimes my dreams are sweet and scented with the cherry and apricot blossoms of my youth. But always there is dying; my Mother, your Mother, and the countless nameless faces I killed during the war.

I cannot kill the slightest living creature that moves, yet every-one who has touched me has shattered like glass."

I kick the empty wine bottle aside and I realize I'm as old as suf-fering itself. To the left of me, across the stream, a wildly colored bird breaks the stagnancy of living with a joyous, hopeful, alleluia. The smell of the stream in its greenness and damp, dark brown earth is witness to my ability to turn the tensions of living into a quiet, cushioned comfort, a communal exchange with my essence. The primal essence and its source is renewed. My consciousness, heightened by the wildness in nature, enables me to perceive my organic and cosmic place in Nature, the Gypsy, and the World.

Orlando Romero

Confession

and Penitence ≡

There is the echoing, thundering, ear-destroying pounding of the flour mill, powered by the Tres Ritos Stream. This was my Grandfather's mill before he moved to Nambé. He knew milling so well that when he moved to Nambé he took an old Casey tractor and conveyed its power into the energy he needed for the mill which he bought somewhere in the Rio Grande Valley. Once in Nambé he continued to grind the corn and wheat of the peoples' farms. Indians from Cochiti to Taos brought him wheat until the day they stopped planting it.

It all reminded me that times are not forgotten, only conveyed by energy and words spoken. Memories set the air on fire, sometimes making us smile with wonder and sometimes making us cry because we know that somewhere, way back, a knot was placed in the wood of our hearts.

Somewhere, on the north slope of a mountain, where winter snows refuse to be melted by the heat of June, here in Tres Ritos, a Penitente walks and haunts the valleys that are drenched with green and magenta. His feet bleed as the sharpness of the jagged stones penetrate his vulnerable skin. His back bleeds. The stones, like the slashing whip on his back, soothe the torment in his soul with little rivulets of blood. He was, and is, then and now, in one form of penitence or another, my Brother, my Father, my Mother, my ancestral blood.

Here along this mountain stream, the camping is but an excuse for being close to the stars. My children and wife are their nucleus.

Only in the constant companionship of memory do I wonder where the Gypsy is now. Her back bent forward, she carries the burdens of the world on her shoulders. But she is strong. Like St. Christopher, she carries her burden across the deep and swift current of life.

It could be she is up there, that constellation with the bear. Shining brightly, she will not falter. She is my wife, my Mother, my Sister and my lover. And in her belly she carries and nourishes her infertile fertility. I have loved them all, from the faintest glow to the brightest fire. She is the hope for mankind. Woman is all the stars in the heavens, and without her gentility and fire, man wanders the road in a pale blue suit, cold and undernourished.

Thunder roars like a black lion and the sky is covered with lightening streaks of pale blue and discolored white. Our tent wants to fly up from its chains as the wind begins to shake the forest. Pine cones fall. Grass bends and sways as the rain begins to pelt my face. Its strength caresses and nourishes the skin that knew morning dew before there was morning dew.

Inside the tent the glow from the kerosene lamp throws playful and warm shadows of yellow and gold on my wife's brown face and body.

The children sleep with dreams that lie in open pastures and trees blossoming with fruit. Because my soul is with the child and the ancient, I dream with them.

Orlando Romero

Up the cherry tree I climb. The ripest, virginal cherry is at the top of the world, surrounded by green sensual leaves. In wisps of dreams and tastes of nectar, honey and apricots, I place my hand on my wife's breast. Her lips emanate heat. Kissing her neck and then her breasts, I become the brownness of her nipples. Our bodies rhythmically quiver, as the arrow that once touched and matures all the world's fruit is released. Between her garden of wildly colored sighs she strokes and enjoys the trespass I have made. With her loving consent, the trespasser has been rewarded with the joy of her hot and nourishing fruit. We become one with energy.

And in that energy the Penitente's whip howls. He has turned his soul upside down. And not until his confession is completed, up there on that slope, will he find himself right side up again.

From memories of glowing candles and dripping wax, dreams cover the walls of the tent.

It is the week before Easter and the confessional line dwarfs my small age and size. My compatriots in crime, mischief, and living are scattered throughout the line that leads into the priest's cave. My friend, Ignacio, twitches in his nervousness. He has been told the priest will give him a severe tongue lashing for his deep, dark sins. His mother behind him is the guarantee that he will bend his knees and confess his youthful, trivial sins.

Now I wait in darkness. Vaguely I can hear the confession of the young woman who went before me. But I do not hear. Everything, like this darkness, is secret here. The pulsating of my heart pounding at the wonder and mystery of this darkness is the only reality I can grasp.

The priest pushes the small, sliding panel.

"Bless me, Father, for I have sinned. It has been weeks since I've been to confession. I have seen, done, touched, laughed at, been angry with _____. And _____."

It is a form, and it is a ritual. Like howling at the moon, dancing to tambourines and violins, or like my hands carving wood. It is not less for me now, only the form is different. My confessions these days are spent in talking and howling at the moon and the stars, in reflecting upon my essence, and in considering the natural energy we humans believe is God.

My friend the atheist is dead. A long time ago he discovered there was no God. He died because he closed himself to the possibility that God just might be. I am alive and well, not because of one God, but many.

Sometimes the Gypsy doubts her own beliefs, and her sorrow is intensified.

Digging ≡—

≡ "Mateo! Leave those bones alone."

We were digging the trench to connect the water from my Sister's house to our new well. Grandfather and I came upon ashes, darkened earth, and a multitude of potsherds. Immediately I had him stop all his work, suspecting that we had come upon a burial mound. As I carefully dug around the site, the entire burial chamber became apparent.

Working on my knees, I stopped to see him approach the site. He blocked the brightness of the noonday sun with his face. I couldn't really see it, only the radiant heat of the sun around it. But through the brightness I could tell he had become indignant. This time his words were harder.

"Mateo! Leave those bones alone!"

"But Grandfather, there is an entire burial here, and it would be a sin not to remove these bones and preserve them for the museum."

In the stunning brightness of the sun, the same sun of Nambé that has nourished countless ancient peoples, he lifted his arm and pointed to our house. In that instant he became part of the sun.

"They are preserved enough. Museum! No seas pendejo! When this house was raised, as well as many of the houses that were built here in Nambé, the foundations holding adobes were detoured so that not a single Indian bone was disturbed. In your Uncle's house alone, there must be at least ten cadavers underneath the floorboards. In our house there is an Indian buried in every other corner."

≒≓

This may have been five years ago, but the recollection comes as a haunting memory reminding me of my scientific search into my ancestral past. The bones and pots had been taken. The few that didn't crumble, after being disturbed and the nocturnal rhythm broken, were carried off in marked paper sacks indicating all sorts of scientific data.

In my Grandfather's eyes, I had perpetuated a wanton rape and with the strength of our plowhorse he stood helpless. He could do nothing to stop my thirst in pleasing the dull scientific picking and digging into the bones of my ancestors.

Orlando Romero

Las Fiestas de Santa Fe
y la Conquistadora ≡

"Andale, niña, give her the wild alfalfa."

"But Daddy, she'll bite my fingers."

Today, this is my most lingering fiesta; my children, goats and Nambé. Within this circle, the gentle goat and her kids are the mountain spirits that live with us.

Weeks before, I had to sell the other goat that carried three kids in her belly. The pack of dogs that roam the nearby hills had previously devoured my chickens, ducks, ducklings and baby roosters. I had chosen to sell her to someone else rather than to see her destroyed before my eyes by the pack. They run in packs, as many as ten or fifteen, here in Nambé. Domestic dogs, harmless while the light of sun is bright, treacherous and destructive while the moon is concealed in the clouds.

In the Barrios, where my people don't own the land, the pack comes at all hours.

In some houses the ancianos sign contracts on the dotted line for cooking utensils, encyclopedias, or Bibles they don't need. Underneath a bridge, a wino clutches his bottle. In a city park, the veins swell up, marking the spot where the needle will tear the flesh, sending its false hope to enslave the soul. In the Barrios, as in the caves, my brothers' expressions will surface in murals, and colors will brighten and shock. The nakedness of elongated, strong brown arms that seem to come out of the dirty city pavement will give color to our joy and suffering for our souls are the color of mountain streams, fish, and wild deer.

It is true. Many of us have lost our lands. For the people in the Barrios the earth of Nambé, Las Trampas, Taos or Pecos may only be a vague memory. But my Grandfather tells me that an ember never dies until the faintest glow leaves the heat of the ashes. Perhaps the people in the Barrios will refuse to be absorbed by the Detroit whore on wheels who leaves a bad-tasting, transient kiss.

But tonight there will be joyous howling at the moon. Here in Nambé, the evening is serene and cool. In my young heart, the sixteen passes over my chin as I shave represent my youth in years that know patience as a curse. Soon they will be here. Six splashes of after-shave. One more comb. The old truck's horn breaks the stare into the mirror wherein I saw myself dancing with her on the plaza tonight.

With my friends and two six-packs we arrive to music of the golden horns. It is hot and sensual, and in the crowd a man in his fifties releases a holler and howl that only people close to the earth can hear and experience. His joy and his agony inspire the Mariachis to further heights and pitches of melody and sensuality.

She is over there, with her friends. I've told my friends we should meet at the truck at one, no later. It can't be later than that. My Mother worries about me and she'll sit up until I return. Her voice echoes.

"Be careful, Mateo. Here, have another peso. Be careful with the gangs in town. And with the girls, be careful. And if they drive fast, you tell them you want to get off. Come home early."

$$\Longrightarrow\Longleftarrow$$

"Look, Mateo, they are landing on the moon."

I get up. The hospital room, shared with another cancer victim, is nauseating with the heaviness of opiates. My mother is dying and, for the first time, this country is landing on the moon.

That seems so long ago. My father's breath was fresh. He returned home to die, but ironically he returned to comfort the dying. With some form of reserved courage, during my mother's last year, he managed to bury her without touching the stuff.

"Look, Mateo, they've landed."

I returned to hold her dying hand. It seems that what she suffers I, too, must share. But it's a good night for landing on the moon.

"Goodnight Mamá, I'll be okay. Please don't wait up for me. It's time for fiestas, I'll be alright."

The street lights around the plaza capture the mood. The glow and aura radiate in the atmosphere. Tonight the moon will sit on top of Santa Fe, it will not set. The moon is the mistress of ritual. She guards her domain with unflinching determination. These are her people, night people. Fed by the sun and now stolen for a brief, pulsating interlude with the mysteries of her own conception, she will show her approval by forcing the sun gods to remain asleep.

"Hello, Bernarda, how are Fiestas? Let me buy you a Coke?"

She walks with me and in me. The power of her essence is the intoxicant that fills my nostrils with fire. Her long brown hair touches her waist and seems to lick her hips. Her little breasts stand firm and erect and she sways with the woman that surfaces in her walk. Her green eyes are as playful as the mood. She greets me with the care and sincerity of innocence.

"I'm glad to see you, Mateo. I was afraid you weren't coming. Would you like to walk with me to the Cathedral? I promised a visit during Fiestas."

"Yes, Bernarda, I would love to."

She took my arm and we walked silently, staring into the depths of each other's eyes. The Mariachis, the laughter, singing, dancing and bodies close and pushing, hard and erect in the crowded streets, heightened our slow procession to the Cathedral. The massive doors were kept open as if constant swallowing was expected or was symbolic of the ritual. The scene inside was cold and warm. Heat radiated from the crucified Christ and from the black shawled old women who ached in their bones from the long hours of meditation into countless Novenas and Rosarys. Images of my Grandmother on my mother's side arose with the smell of melting, dripping wax. The long hours of abstinence before Communion as a child stirred up the chocolate memories that I believed to be dead. In the memory of the meaningful, nothing ever dies.

Bernarda genuflected. The coldness of the lavish surroundings dampened my adobe spirit. To the left side of the main altar stood La Conquistadora. She gazes into the void. She is historical, venerated, and yet she can't see me. The adobe of my soul is dampened and the dreaded rivulets of rain wash at the primal elemental essence. The Indian is invoked and a frenzy of numbness arises.

The Conquistadora of Whom? Is this the Perpetuator of the coldness that haunts this Cathedral?

"To take Possession by violent means."

In a few hours she will be paraded in the streets. A holy, religious procession. The lady we pray to, before she saved us from the Indians she was Christ's mother. And I'm tossed about in confusion. Why is it the Indian blood in us can allow her to take on the attributes of a conqueror?

"Mateo, what's the matter? You look so sad; pray for me and peace. Look, Saint Francis is surrounded by the birds and animals of our fields."

I am renewed. She believes and her belief is that of kindness, love and peace; and with St. Francis, the solitude and strength that is in his aura, she is the strength I need to see me through confusion.

We leave the paradox of the Cathedral. The tantalizing smell of green chile and the various New Mexican dishes being prepared on the plaza fill us with a hunger that comes from the physical closeness to our own fields and plants.

"Mateo, in the Cathedral . . . you looked different. You looked so old. You scared me. You looked older than my Grandfather."

To answer her would be to confuse her and bring back memories of a night I'm not quite sure existed. I change the subject because it is natural for human beings to go on living.

"Look over there, Bernarda! That looks like a good place to eat. That group cooking is from our valley."

And she smiles with the smoothness of her skin and the glow of her eyes under the watchful moon. We eat, drink, and talk with the laughter that is in our age. We talk of the dance concert we'll be going to, a popular rock and roll group is coming to Santa Fe especially for Fiestas. The pounding of their drums is supposed to evoke a primitive frenzy in our souls. But, in me, memories are evoked at the slightest suggestion of earth smells, dark, mysterious nights, and eyes that constantly search for me in the crowd.

It is a dark night. My Brother is somewhere behind me. Soon we will reach my Uncle's house.

I shout in the moonless night, as if my young person were a cry from an eternally lost lifeboat.

"Miguel, hurry! Soon we will have to go by the Campo Santo."

My shout echoes, but my Brother's voice does not follow. Where is my Brother?

In the Campo Santo, the wooden crosses, in their almost tribal designs, release splinters that fly at me in the darkness and terrify my youthful spirit. I ponder and stumble in the stagnant air, suffocating with the smell of souls tossing and turning. They call out and reach for mortals who are afraid of death.

My Brother's voice breaks the stillness.

"Mateo, did you hear her? La Llorona, she's looking for her lost children! She's haunting the Campo Santo! Hurry, let's go! She'll get us! Come on! What's the matter?"

I can't move, I am in a state of paralysis. Miguel has fled in fear. I can't see or feel, cold numbness is all around me.

Voices; crying. I hear wild laughter and the maddening galloping of horses, then the creaking of heavy wooden carts.

The air is broken by whips slashing the air in drops of blood.

I hear something like music. It is a Penitente pito, haunting and transforming my numbness into a state of sleep.

Green eyes. A black shawl. I feel the presence of a soul at ease, but is it real or is it in sleep that we are haunted?

"Mateo, don't be afraid. I'm your Grandmother, the one who never held you close to her breast or stroked your fine, dark brown hair or sang 'A ROO A ROO' to you. I am a spirit. Do not be afraid my child, my soul rests in peace and will not haunt your dreams. When you last came to see me, with your Grandfather, and he cried as you placed flowers on my grave, I couldn't speak to you for fear of frightening you. But your Grandfather knows. Mateo, you're almost a man. Soon you will begin to feel alone because you'll see, feel, hear, touch, and breathe ideas and things few can conceive. Accept it now, so that your life won't be filled with confusion and doubt. It is not a curse, it is a gift."

⇒⇐

Ta-Ta-Ta, Ta, Ta, Ta, Ta-Ta-Ta. Golden musical reflections from Mariachis' horns push Bernarda and I further into the crowd. With the swaying, exotic melody in an enormous circle and the clasping, clinging of hands to each other, Bernarda and I dance. With skirts flying up to heaven and Spanish filigree jewelry sparkling like the stars, the heat of the dancing people turns into the golden color the tiger lost as he chased his shadow around the ever elusive moon.

Once again, the old man with the paper sack takes a drink from his endless Fiesta well. He holds his sack in the air, straightens and lets the world know he is alive and whole by letting out a wild holler that amuses the tourists. It is the cry of the revolution he was never in or won, the woman he never had, and the joy of being able to tell God and the moon he's still going to live a long time . . . even if he dies tomorrow.

There, in the crowd, are many Gypsies, but we do not see or hear them because tonight we all sing, cry and dance.

Tea ≡

≡ The Gypsy smiles and her glow fills the room. Her green eyes are mine now. I hold them tightly between the lifelines of my palm. She, too, holds my eyes. She keeps them in a niche under her pillow. In the darkest night we see with each other's eyes and memories.

Tonight while December's wind and snows freeze the brown of the ground, she is busy preparing a cup of tea.

"Mateo, have you ever had this kind of tea before?"

"No, but it smells good. Like oranges and spices."

Pausing as if she was not quite sure, or if somewhere in her memory someone had told her she was the mother of the earth herbs and teas, she said: "It does have orange bits and comes from a far away land."

The wind howls, but the adobe of her house becomes our womb. The essence of her tea, smiles, and hair has turned the air of the room into a magical, pulsating circus tent that burns in orange and black. But the tiger sleeps tonight. In waves of a faraway aphrodisiac, his slumber will turn to dreams.

She smiles as we sit. She in her royal oaken chair and I, at her feet. We sip as if this were the last nourishment that the last two people on earth are to have. The gentle ritual is blessed by the honey of her skin and hair.

In a floating state of magical enchantment with the flames of love licking our very words, actions and thoughts, I hear my words penetrate the armor of her soul.

"What else is in this tea, sweet lady?"

"My dreams of love and life, spiced by your company."

And she tries running, reaching, searching for the words she's almost accidentally let escape.

But it is in our magic, in our auras and in our souls that we constantly find the beauty of truth and peace. We have no reason to lie. We know and are each other.

In sips of threes our mouths and lips have touched. In the magic of her tea I have become her dancing bear. We have camped at the edge of town but in an instant's notice we will travel the roads of the world. I will perform for her, for us, and I will protect our secret. No one dares question my Gypsy's secret.

So tonight we sip our tea, but even more, we will drink from each other's fountain the cool spring water of each other's forgotten memories.

While the heat of her cat's purr reaches our ears I lay my head in the greenness of memory between her breasts. Here I hear and feel the pounding of her heart and the river that runs wild with love. When the high water has decreased she will have fertilized my soil.

Followed by the star at the tip of a quarter moon, we dance in each other's eyes.

Those gazing, longing, lonely eyes of hers . . . green as emeralds, mountain pools. They follow me in the brightest sun. They dance in the darkness of day, cry at the lateness of life, green eyes, smiling kindness of the child that is a woman.

Followed by the flight of a falling star, I trace the middle and the corners of her mouth. Mother goddess, evoker of Salamanders, serpents, star-filled nights, suspended moons, and dying suns, she holds and embraces me lovingly.

She rises for a second cup of tea and walks with the joy and confusion that is her secret. But I, Mateo Romero, the great, great, great grandson of the first hybrid, solar-maize plant blood, see her joy and suffering. Her terribly curious inquisitiveness into the mysteries of living and dying are her salvation.

Tonight, in her tea, my words, in the aura of our magic and the mystical blueness of these mountains that exists despite the snow, she will begin to reflect and question her fears. From tonight on she will ask the stars for answers. She will consult her high priest; she's been to him before.

In the movement of her graceful hands she will follow and be saddened by the fears she has finally dared question. She could be free, liberated, lonely, contemporary woman, but the seed that is in her womb is ancient. She can't deny the heat and gentleness of her womanhood. In the movement of her long, lovely graceful hands, she will pull me closer to her, then away from her.

Orlando Romero

Letters in a Chest

October 18, 1863

My Dear Gentle Lady,

In three weeks a tea merchant on a gray mule will be stopping at your place of residence in Santa Fe. I described your affliction; he told me that your worries could be solved with his magical herbs and teas. Here in Mexico City he is known as a doctor of wild weeds.

So that there be no mistake in identifying his person, the following description should be of some assistance.

He is of average height though his stature is shadowing. Like his people, he is of dark complexion, but there is a tinge of gold in his color. His eyes are green and quite enchanting. His hands are quite large and deeply sunburned. The color of his hair is like a moonless night.

There is a strange aura about him, especially when he speaks. A certain calm and mystery are part of his words. In

the village I passed through yesterday, I was told, his father was
an Indian High Priest. I do know he carries a small statue of a
black Virgin in his travels.

I expect to settle this matter of the horses soon. Hoping to
find you in excellent spirits and await the smile on your lips, I
close with love and a longing soul.

Juan López Romero

The aromatic essence and spell of an ancient, hand-hewn cedar chest, with bright silver buckles and my tiger-yellow and orange cat, are my companions and keys that open a forgotten world my great grandparents knew as their times.

My Great Grandmother tied all his letters with an orange velvet ribbon. The chest is full of treasures and sparkle that come to life every time I sneak up to the attic.

"Mateo! Mateo, where are you? Are you up in the attic again? Leave that chest alone! Do you hear me up there? Don't eat that meat up there, it's not dry yet."

"I'm up here, Mamá. I'm just looking at all these old things, I'll be down in just a minute!"

"You better, muchacho! You've got to take the Holy Family to the Salazars, it's their turn this week."

=≡≡

Someone is picking a guitar very gently and then very rapidly. There are feet stomping on polished hardwood floors.

"¡Arriba, arriba, arriba, mujer! ¡Baila conmigo! ¡Andale mujer, dame tu mano!"

My cat's ears pick up. They, too, have heard the wild musical language. It's coming from the chest.

"Go on . . . go your way vaquero, I don't care to dance with you!"

But the vaquero pleads truth, sincerity and a brave boast.

"Por favor, Señorita. I'm the best dancer in this county and surely you are the most beautiful lady in the world. Look, all the señoritas are looking this way, wondering when I'm going to show them how to click their heels at the moon."

Twirling, hand exchanging, violin pitches skimming across the dance floor, and polished boots stomping the festive notes deep into the foundation of memory whirl around my head, through my very pores and to the center of my very soul. I am my handsome Great Grandfather, the joyous faces dancing, the women sitting together, the groomed, shaved faces of the men, young and old, waiting their turn to dance with their favorite partner. Husbands, wives, sons, daughters, lovers and dreamers: they all dance.

My forehead is moist with the heat and energy of being alive. She clings closely to me. It seems as if we are dancing on a rolling meadow all by ourselves, only the butterflies dance with us.

"Señorita, tonight we will dance our way to the grave. Let the stars fall and we will dance on them too."

She hears and understands and is not afraid. She knows tonight will be their first night and with the strength and callouses of his hands, the brave bold words, and the sorrow in his eyes, she will remember no other man as lingering sweetness and gentleness.

$$=\!\!=\!\!\Longleftarrow$$

The music ends and the cedar wood returns to my nostrils. I pet my cat and he begins to purr. Under the spell, I open another letter.

August 21, 1862

Querida Flor,

I beg you forgive the boldness and intrusion of this letter. In all truth I am, or have become, incapable of addressing you vocally. I have seen you in Mass twice since we last danced, but as usual, when I was ready to speak my soul burst and my tongue shriveled.

I have seen your lovely eyes in glances, hidden glances, all meant for me. Behind the lace, gentle lady, do you search and try to recapture what your eyes say to me?

Loving me is at times difficult, but full of joy, passion, gentle hours and lingering memories. You know what they call me, 'Turko'! Don't believe it.

It is true that my soul is burdened with the sensitivity to the music from these fields and my swift wild horses, but, gentle lady, what good is it to me if no one can share or see the poetry of living and dying?

It is you, wild flower, trust in the power and magic of my love and you will inspire me to heights above our tallest peaks. All I ask is that you consider me and the possibility of allowing your soul to lay by mine.

Juan López Romero

Orlando Romero

La hembra es la puerta
a los misterios del universo ═━

═━ "Mamá, Mamá, when are we going to be finished?"
With both of us on our knees scrubbing the rich doctor's floors,
she turns to free me.

"Ahorita, mi'jito . . . ahorita."

Then, as if she didn't have me to talk to at that instant of loneliness, when her need was greatest for releasing the troubles in her
soul, she paused. To this day I still wonder if she was talking to me.

"Look at me on my knees. We used to dance as if the morning
would never appear. I guess it must be God's will, but sometimes I
just don't understand how He works things."

Looking into my eyes as if there were some answers there she
asked, "Where is he now? Not a letter, not a question about us. I
wonder what occupies his time?"

With the reassurance of her childhood memories, she reminisces.

"I remember when I was a young girl and we used to go to the
dances at the hall here in Nambé. On a cool spring evening we
used to walk past the church and all the wonderful smells of the

earth and Nambé filled my nostrils as if I were being excited by the young colt in your Grandfather's pasture. Everything then seemed so magical! I was young and the cool spring air would turn my cheeks red and the dew would wash my lips. Your Father used to call me 'Lady of the Rain.' He was a very handsome man, then, and he hardly ever drank. He used to spend his time reading books. I had never heard or dreamed of those books. He used to write me the nicest words. They filled my head with dreams and made me feel sort of special because he could think of me that way."

Then, pausing from the heaviness of memories drunk to oblivion by forces that can't be foretold, she said, "Mateo, when you marry you dance with your woman, give her love, and stand beside her and you'll remember your Mamá as a smiling 'Lady of the Rain.' Don't hate your Father, I don't. Have faith and you'll live a long time."

Orlando Romero

Nubes ≡

In the pelting rain I saw my Mother's petunias melt into the brownness of the earth. Nambé receives its life and passion from the sun. It rains little here. When it does rain, the inhabitants and dwellers of this ancient place take on different appearances. The forehead of the face hangs obtrusively on the brow. The color of living complexion turns gray like the sky and the eye sockets turn black like the storm. The gentleness is replaced by the heaviness of darkened spirits. It shows in their movements. Sparks fly at the darkened skies.

Viable, reflexive, warm muscles are now trapped in cages. Their adobe house, or womb, is warm. But they look out with longing eyes and tired sighs; their goats, cows, horses and plows sit unmoving. In one day's rain the soul of these inhabitants will begin to gather rust.

I sit by the corner fireplace, watching the piñon flames burn the air around them. My cat purrs in his dreams. His tail switches, then his leg. He dreams of the cat next door.

Here in Nambé, we all dream. Some of us in the middle of the sun, some of us under black storms. My Grandfather dreams as he nervously paces the floor. He longs for his fields.

My Mother sits on the rocking chair in the corner. She's looking at her book pretending she is reading. In reality, she dreams. Her smile is warm and gentle. Her eyes are lonely and longing, and though her body is young and strong she always looks tired. She works hard. Whenever I can, I help her clean the rich doctor's house and the other millionaires' houses that are scattered throughout the valley.

They say they like to live like us. Adobe houses, corner fireplaces, vigas and all the other materials that surround us. They, too, like our "charm." The essence they will never see; the living and dying of it they will never feel. Some don't care to. There are exceptions; the doctor's wife is gentle, kind and understanding. She reminds me of my Mother.

In dreams of gentle smiles, with piñon flames licking the foundation of memory and the warmth of our adobe womb I dream in the longing of my Mother's thoughts.

$$\Longrightarrow\Longleftarrow$$

"How am I so wrong for him? He drinks and drinks. I don't make him happy. He finds no peace here at home. I wonder how he's doing in California? Six months now, not a word. Doesn't he realize he's my only man. No one kisses my breasts, no one talks to me in the lateness of the evenings, no man makes me laugh like he does. That first year, it was so fine, so rich and gentle. What distracted him? Why can't he raise himself above it, instead of drinking himself below it?"

In her longing glances and the warmth of our fire, I wonder where my Father is. My memories of him are mixed between the good and the confused. No one takes me fishing up to the beaver ponds now, or lets me shoot the twenty-two. I wonder what California is like? Why doesn't he send me a pocket knife or a yo-yo, like he said he would?

Denying memory and the sorrow that haunts, not realities but appearances, illusions, and what appears to be the surface of auras, I ask my Grandfather to tell me a story.

"Grandpa, tell me a story, when you were little like me, when you lived in Las Trampas with your goats."

His pacing stopped, the color of the sun returned to his face because there was nothing that brought him more joy than to remember his childhood. He walked to the old trastero he had carved. From it he took a piece of dried meat for both of us. Then with his enormous golden and calloused hands he gestured for me to move so that we could both sit on the adobe banco near the corner fireplace.

In his closeness to me, his presence was as soothing as the ancient herbal medicines he put into his words.

"Let's see, have I told you about the time we had a billy goat with four horns and what happened to me with a descanso?"

"No, what's a descanso, Grandpa?"

"You know what a descanso is. You see them on the highway all the time. A descanso is a cross marking the place where a person has died."

"You mean where he is buried, Grandpa?"

"No, no, it just marks the place where a person has died. Listen carefully to me, Mateo, I know you may forget because there have been times when I've been reckless with the things I should have remembered."

In his pause he glanced outside the window. The storm might end after his story.

"Anyway I was about your age and my Father had given me charge of forty or fifty goats. Among them we had a wild and strange billy goat. From the day he was born he was strange. His mother had never been with another male or macho before, yet she still had him, and stranger yet, as he grew older there appeared four horns on his head, instead of two. He was more than mischievous, most of the time we had to keep him locked up in the pen by himself. One day he almost broke your Great Grandfather's ribs. He butted unexpectedly and from that day on we were warned he might kill one of us with his strength and cunning. But, because those days were full of strange and mysterious things around us, we thought nothing of it. Yet, we always respected him."

Between the battle of the jerky and his old teeth, my Grandfather continued the story.

"Well, one day, I took the herd of goats with the billy goat about three miles from our home, up to a high valley plateau. Here the pasture was tall and there was a stream that cut the green valley in halves. It was like a green emerald. It was full of peace and calm with the birds and noises of summer stinging the stillness of the air with music.

"The goats were browsing peacefully, but, like goats, we never stayed in one place very long. The billy goat was peaceful enough that day and I could always tell where he was, just by his smell. I did think it was kind of unusual that he was so calm. Everything, in reality, was much too calm. There seemed to exist a timeless flickering green sense of being totally caught in a suspended dream. I began to tire, so I took out my pocketknife and started to carve a small Santo on an old weathered cottonwood root. But my age being what it was, I glanced around for more daring adventures, maybe some carving on something unusual.

"My eyes scanned the nearby piñon trees, and the twisted roots that seemed determined to cling to life, though some of them were only embracing barren rocks. I searched the hideously wind-formed limbs of junipers that reminded me of La Llorona's arms in her desperate, longing search for children that might never have been hers. These weren't the target for my pocket knife. Instead, my restless childish eyes focused on a tall descanso. Larger than

Orlando Romero

most descansos, it was sawed and carved in the old way of carving crosses, intricate forceful designs, with swirls pointing down as if the soul might still be on the spot where it began its flight, stopped to dream, and its physical house destroyed.

"Instantly I expected a delightful thrill as I uprooted the descanso; my knife could hardly wait to put its own designs on it. Instead, the peaceful, glowing emerald of the valley was ripped apart by a lightning bolt eight or ten feet away from me. The sun disappeared into what seemed to be an intensely black crack in the sky. The goats cried as if they were being slaughtered by a dull knife. I stood terrified, numb and paralyzed in the fear that swept the valley and my soul. Maybe it lasted a minute, it felt more like a hundred years. I thought I was never going to see it again, but the sun burst through the darkness and again returned the peace and green of the emerald to the valley.

"Having been reborn, I searched for my scattered goats. I searched till it was nearly dark, fearing the whipping I was going to get for having lost the herd. I knew it was useless to search in the dark, so, exhausted, I returned home.

"There in the open pen, as well as I could tell by the falling light, were all my goats. The smell of the billy goat with the four horns still lingered, yet somehow I knew he wasn't there. Besides, he was so large his silhouette always towered above the rest of the goats. My father asked me the reasons for all the commotion, the goats running at breakneck speed and the loss of the billy goat, and my tired, dirty, old man appearance.

"When I told him about the descanso, that was as far as I had to go. He took me by the arm, took the piece of leather strap that tied the gate and was about to whip my pants when my mother caught his arm in the air. 'No,' she said, 'leave him alone. You can tell, he'll never forget it for as long as he lives.'

"Next day we got up even earlier than usual. We searched every ravine, arroyo, crevice and canyon in that valley. We never found trace of the goat with the four horns. No blood, no tracks, no struggle; it just disappeared to where it came from."

"But Grandpa, where did it go? Maybe he was the devil, Grandpa? I don't understand!"

"Understand, understand, don't be like the Americanos, they have to understand everything. It was a lesson, a miracle or a mystery. Just believe in mysteries, and you'll live a long time."

At the trail of his words, the sun broke through the storm clouds of Nambé. He looked up at the remaining clouds and said, "Estas nubes, siempre me siguen pero no les vale mojarme."

Orlando Romero

Lilacs ≡—

≡ Along with the morning blossoms I had picked for the Gypsy, my soul found within the heart-shaped leaves of the lilac these words:

> *Because every time you leave me, you leave the*
> *essence of apricot, apple and lilac blossoms, and*
> *because your soul needs blossoms in the springs*
> *and summers of its years, I've brought you these.*

I placed them at her doorstep. Then I ran with the wind so that my male spirit would not disturb her dreams. It must have been seven-thirty in the early spring or summer, when the ancient earth sighs in morning slumber with memories of countless colorful, blossoming seasons of illusions. It is in the early morning hours that the sun dazzles through her window, through everyone's window, caressing our childhood memories that were nourished and created in the bed of sleep and dreams.

She turns gently on her pillow with her soft hair imitating the caress of a gentle, newborn, sweet-scented breeze. Have I disturbed her dreams or are we each other's dreams? Is that the bond of our love? We realize that some dreams end with abrupt awakenings.

It was at her doorstep, in the middle of winter, that a small snow-filled man melted. He disappeared into the flagstones by her door. His little pebble eyes remained along with the same warm smile that caused him to melt. There in the middle of a cruel physical winter, the bronze, golden sun of Nambé penetrated and perpetuated the solitude of enigmas that constitute living in the land of ancient ghosts and paradoxes. Like he was never there, and as if he were a different form of energy, he melted and disappeared. Only the memory lingers, always memory. It stays behind and sometimes jumps ahead of time, which we consider more valuable than wealth.

That seems to be only fleeing minutes and seconds, now I find her, under her cape, carrying the burden of my flowers. Her flowers too. She has watched them grow and watered them with the laughter in my eyes.

Because she loves me as much as she is afraid of herself she asks questions to which the answers are within her.

"Mateo, why did you bring me flowers this morning?"

"I thought you'd like them."

Her round, mother-goddess face was alive with the countless creatures of love expressing themselves in her eyes and on her mouth.

"Yes, I do like them, they are beautiful, but you made me cry. Mateo, I don't want you to tell me that you love me. Because I know you do. That alone is sufficient burden."

I responded, but only with echoes. I knew I was repeating ancient words said at altars, mountain tops, river valleys and the many places where our Mother has been worshipped.

"Gentle Lady, shall I deny my soul by dropping it down the canyons of Cordova? You are the center of this universe and countless others."

Orlando Romero

The corners of her mouth are wet, sprayed by the sea, though the only seas that exist in Northern New Mexico are those living at the instant of creation. In the vast and limitless expanse of that illusionary sea, her mouth portrays the reality of the loneliness of a profundity whose essence lies in the alienation produced by its overwhelming immensity.

I reached for her hand because in her mystical, magical, magnetic eyes she reached for me.

Her hand was soft and the long gentle fingers that always expressed the woman in her soul played with my lifelines. She transformed my hand into a melodious harp only a bewitching siren could play. Its music passed through my wrists, past my elbows and into the most vulnerable chamber of my being, my poetic soul.

Then she hushed my lips and my thoughts with those same gentle fingers.

"Mateo, there are things about me you don't understand. Look into my eyes, Mateo, I don't want to hurt you with them."

She saddened and I knew the essence of the flowers and the lilacs was disappearing and wilting. I couldn't tell her that I did understand and that it didn't matter.

La Bartola or La Llorona? ≡

≡ She had no one to talk with. Yet many people in Nambé said they could hear her howling at the moon. It was true that during moon flooded nights she was seen walking the brown earth and gray mesas of Nambé with her seven wild dogs.

They said she lived by herself. Her house was almost a landmark, the way it stood by itself between Nambé pueblo and Nambé village. She looked like her adobe house. It was so weathered by time that most of the mud plaster was cracking and the wood of the windows had turned a soft, wild nappy gray.

I was on my way to the waterfalls, with my fishing rod in hand, when I saw her for the first time. Walking near her house, the pack of dogs charged. She rushed out to calm her dogs and at first sight I almost died of fear. Her hair was wild and straight, between silver gray and sun bleached white. It was like the colorless cadavers and animal skulls that seem lost to the ties of living, which in reality have been blessed to white by natural sterilization. She wasn't ugly, but her stature and physical appearance was beyond comprehension. After she barked, and talked to her dogs and convinced them I should be left alone, I had a better opportunity to look at her more closely.

It looked like she was wearing a misshapen gunny sack with old wrinkled boots protruding from within and beneath the hem. The top that covered the strange dress looked like an old fashioned leather vest. It was a faded purple as if irises had died on it.

Her skin was brown like her adobe house and just as cracked. Her hands were thorny and calloused. Yet in all this chaos, shouting and barking, there was such a strange aura of peace coming from her wild green eyes that I wasn't sure if my life had been threatened at all by the pack of wild dogs.

As she opened her mouth and her parched lips parted I saw her ancient earth stained teeth. Even in my boyish body and mind I wondered who had been her lover.

"Little boy, what are you doing here? Where are all your friends, the ones who throw eggs at my windows and taunt my dreams and my solitude?"

I almost cried because, as she barked at me, she began to look like her wild dogs.

"Well, what do you want with me?"

As a tear rolled down my face and my knees quivered, she reached her gnarled hand for my shoulder.

"No, no, little boy, don't cry."

I was so terrified that I broke out in sobs. She took a dirty old rag from underneath her sack and wiped my eyes and told me to blow my nose.

Turning to her dogs she said, "Now see what I've done because of you, I've turned this child to tearful butter."

Unexpectedly she pulled me towards her and put my head between her sagging breasts. I smelled the sweat of the earth and felt the coarseness of her dress and in my closeness I felt the gentle flutter of her beating heart. It was soft and sweet, like the cooing of doves.

Looking down at me, with my fishing rod to the side, my hair tangled in her own gray webs and my tears turning to little adobe droplets, she whispered like the wind.

"Hush, hush, niñito. I'm just a lonely old woman."

With the natural poetry of her lifelines and the reassurance of her lonely green eyes, she calmed me.

"Here, come inside, I know what little boys like, some chocolate or some dried meat, eh?"

She gave me some dried venison that she had hunted with her wild dogs. It was the best carne seca I had ever tasted and soon I forgot about fishing. She kept telling me stories and then she talked about herself, not so much with her words as with her lonely green eyes.

"I had a little boy like you once. He had my eyes but his father's hair and features. He grew tall quickly, with strong bones, and had as much energy as the morning sun."

She paused and I thought she was going to stop because the sun was dying and the Sangre de Cristos outside her egg stained windows would soon turn magenta like the aura of her cave.

"But people never left us alone. Snakes' tongues were always whispering, some would shout. They used to taunt him. 'Who was your father, nothing but a wandering Turko.' Manuelito would come running to my arms and ask who his father was and where he was. All I could say was in memory. But Manuelito understood he was the son of a very special man, and was content to hear the stories of his father's deeds and words. In those days men cried like women and women cried like men. But there was also the jealousy of darkness and fear and the countless superstitions of mortals afraid of death. That's why they hated Manuelito, he outlived death and the dark cloud of death never darkened his sky."

She paused as if to make sure and safe, that I, her high priest and confessor, was listening to her every word. When she was convinced I was, she continued.

"In the middle of January, up in Tres Ritos, that's where we lived, a terrible plague terrified all the villages. Little children died every day. No children Manuelito's age were spared. Miraculously, Manuelito, somehow, was spared even the fever. They whispered again. This time they blamed me and my Gypsy son for the curse that had decayed the villages.

We weathered that cruel winter of death, sorrow, and haunting, restless spirits. But in the early spring, after almost being suffocated by the winter, when I was considering moving away from their ruthless tongues, I discovered the fear of loathsome shadows picking away at my soul telling me I was never to have anyone except memory.

Manuelito would spend hours in the canyons and pastures of the high mountains with his beloved goats and kids. One evening Manuelito's goats came home, but Manuelito didn't. In those days children were stolen, some were sold. I wandered up and down the canyons of Tres Ritos wailing till I became hoarse and almost lost my voice, but I never found my beautiful child."

She had me spellbound by her story, and in the darkness on the way home all I could remember was the peace and sorrow in her wild green eyes.

Doña Ana ≡—

≡ Because in all innocence there is truth, and because innocence is pure and childlike, I, sculptor and stumbler into the world
of dreams and illusions once again find myself surrounded by the
voices of children in the middle of a game. We are playing Lady Ana.

With all of us clasping hands and forming a circle, a dark,
green-eyed girl is sitting in the middle of the circle. She is Lady
Ana. While we sing the first and second verse, she will sing the
third, then we will sing the last. And the melody is haunting with
the pungencies of childhood memories when it was easy to live
and accept the world of illusions. Here, in this circle of imagination, Lady Ana will pretend to open a rosebud, close a pink, and eat
parsley as we sing the first two verses. In child-like reality, after the
fourth and last verse, we will question Lady Ana's condition.

Under orange, apricot tree, with the smothering sun of Nambé
determined to sink the sparrow hawk of imagination and dreams,
I float along with the magnetism of childhood memories. The
memories of the music and our young voices is the hallucinogen
that carries my wakeful dreamlike realities. We sing in the circle
of Nambé.

58

Where is the Lady Ana,
Within her garden wall?
A rosebud she is op'ning,
And closing pinks so small.
Come let us go a-strolling,
Just to see what we can see,
I think the Lady Ana
Eats parsley by that tree.

As if little Lady Ana already knew from childhood the limits of solitude, she questions:

Who can these people be
Who pass my house like sheep?
All day and night they wander
And never let me sleep.

With the sweetness of innocence and truth, we explain the interruption of her solitude:

We are the famous students
Who have come to study here;
We come to see the chapel
Of the Virgin Mary dear.

The game is almost ended and the singing has died but my dream, like memories, continues to live like the children's questions in the game:

The Group: How is Lady Ana?
Lady Ana: She has a fever.
The Group: How is Lady Ana?
Lady Ana: She is dying.
The Group: How is Lady Ana?
Lady Ana: She is dead.

Then all the commotion begins. At the end of these words Lady Ana stretches out on the floor and pretends she has died. We all gather around her to see if she is really dead. I, little Mateo Romero, know what will happen next. She will come to life and will try to catch one of us into playing Lady Ana again. But somehow my dream will end before she comes to life again. And I will search for the rest of my life for the rebirth of Lady Ana.

Orlando Romero

Doña Sebastiana ≡

≡ "Arrastrando La Carreta de La Muerte, con sus ruedas amarradas y apretadas el Penitente daba empujos lagrimosos y callados."

≡≡

It was on this Ash Wednesday, like on every other Ash Wednesday since I could remember, that my Grandfather was again repeating the story of the woman who died during a procession of Penitentes. His voice, heavy with the magic of memories, captivated my attention. His Father had told him the tale and both he and I would always live in its echoes.

"With the procession coming closer to the church, a woman was getting closer to the path where the Penitentes' bare feet would announce the silent suffering in their souls. All along the woman had been curious. Was her husband a Penitente? Little did the poor soul realize that it may take more than one lifetime to really know our friends and loves. The Penitente pito wailed in the opaqueness of bluish moonlight as La Carreta de la Muerte with Doña Sebastiana was approaching. The woman whose curiosity had to be satisfied was waiting. Her intentions were to pull aside his hood as the man dragged the death cart in front of her.

"Wait, wait, Grandpa!" I exclaimed, knowing well that last Ash Wednesday I had stopped him at this very same place, as if I was denying the answer, or trying to pretend there might not be an answer. "Who was Doña Sebastiana?"

He was in my blood and he knew well why I was trying to forget the answer to my own question.

"Doña Sebastiana es La Muerte."

And so, to make death in her female apparel understandable, he continued with the mood of that eventful night.

"It didn't take much moonlight to see her face from within the cart. Her color was that of white chalk and her obsidian eyes reflected like black diamonds, despite the hooded and faded black dress that partially covered the sides of her face. It was terrifying. In her outstretched arms she carried and pointed the symbolic bow and arrow. You could tell that the Penitentes as well as the people gathered there were feeling the burden of those cold obsidian eyes staring at them. But this curious, foolish woman who was waiting ignored the stares. As she stretched her arm from underneath her black shawl, there was a terribly cold gust of wind. Everyone there stopped to see her actions. The woman was breaking the natural rhythm of the sufferer and his procession. Foolish, foolish woman. No lover had such competition. The woman was dealing with Doña Sebastiana, the mistress of her man."

In the presence of my Grandfather's mildly righteous and philosophical words, his memory has the power to transport and lead me down the same path where the procession took place. His eyes are wild with the imagination that can be found in the reality of things past.

"It took but an instant, yet that instant brought her such horror that she collapsed to the ground. No one else dared to look at the Penitente when she pulled his hood aside. They knew and respected

Orlando Romero

death. In her dying breaths she had said she'd seen Doña Sebastiana's face where his should have been!"

"What happened to the lady, Grandpa?"

"Mateo, learn to listen closely. Wisdoms are never loud. They come like cool summer breezes and if one doesn't learn to enjoy and live them, they may never appear again."

Then he paused because he knew it was wrong to burden the young with too many words. "Mateo, it is getting late. You'd better go to bed. Tomorrow we have to return life to the fields with the manure that your Uncle gave us."

Lying in the little shepherd's bed that my Grandfather made me, I take refuge from the cold death winds of March wrapped in woolen serapes he has woven on his own loom. Even in my youth I am sleepless. I turn restlessly with my young woes. I see my teacher's face staring at me.

"Mateo, I don't understand. If your grades don't improve I'm going to have a talk with your mother." Then he paused and his stare becomes more intense. "Mateo, you have to speak more English."

> *"Our Father, who art in Heaven, hallowed be Thy*
> *name, Thy kingdom come, Thy will be done, on earth*
> *as it is in Heaven. Give us this day our daily bread*
> *and forgive us our trespasses as we forgive those who*
> *trespass against us and lead us not in temptation,*
> *but deliver us from evil. Amen."*

But it doesn't help, so I reach for my Rosary from underneath the pillow. I concentrate and meditate every bead. I feel so old yet I know I'm only a little boy. Finally, as if intoxicated by the weariness of sleeplessness, I feel myself being turned in the pull of a whirlwind. But I'm not being pulled anywhere. I'm just caught and suspended in the pull of two powerful magnets.

"¡Qué lluvia tan desgraciada!"

Marcos García's words echo in the fathom mist of this unnatural rain on the first week in March. His partner and compadre, Fermin Gonzales, stoically sits beneath his oiled and rain proof rawhide rain slick. Both their horses' pace is caught in the same magnetic pull that traps my dreams and sleep. They barely move in fog that is so rare in Nambé. They hope their horses will lead them to their warm beds and the loving affections of their young brides.

Marcos is disturbed by the eerie mist.

"What time do you think it is, Fermin?"

"God only knows. All I know is that we're somewhere in Nambé and it's 1830." From under his slick he pushes a bottle of home-made wine.

"Here, Marcos, have a drink. It may not keep this chill and mist away, but it will help you ease your worries."

The horses move and they wearily stir in their saddles. With the chill that fills their bones, the longing to be with their women is intensified.

"You know something, Fermin? Every time I'm coming down from those Sangre de Cristos I get the feeling I'll never see my Juanita's green eyes again. I don't care if it's just a week or a couple of days; every time you and I go up there looking for the big bucks I feel that when I get home she won't be there."

"No seas pendejo, Marcos, she's devoted to you and everyone in the village knows how much she loves you. Do you know that my wife caught her picking wild flowers in the fields one day when you were gone to Santa Fe. She told my wife how much you loved flow-ers and that she wanted to smother the house with flowers when you returned."

In the unnatural, incessant mist and chill the horses neigh. Their second fears are more intense as Fermin is almost rocked out of his saddle when his horse's hooves claw the mist in fear. Marcos extends the candlelight lamp. No one is seen, yet someone approaches.

Less than two feet away, like a ghostly apparition, a figure be-comes visible by the dim light of Marcos' lamp. They are stunned

Orlando Romero

beyond belief. The figure is shrouded in a black leather cape. A hood covers all of his face except two bluish specks of light that seem to come from his eyes. They are not sure if he even has eyes. His horse is the blackest horse they have ever seen. Even in the saddle, his height towers above them. Yet, the figure is not as wide as if a man's body lies within the cape and hood. His horse comes between Marcos and Fermin, as if they were not even there, and smoothly glides and eases his way between them. They both notice a black cock, with his bluish-black rain-resistant feathers, peeking its bloody red crown out of his master's cape. The rooster seems to be sitting between his legs. The chill they both knew before has turned to beads of perspiration, and the mist becomes suffocating.

Speechless and almost motionless, Fermin slowly reaches for Marcos' dim lamp. As if in a state of sleep-walking he dismounts. He brings the lamp close enough to the ground to touch it. Fermin's fears find words.

"Dios Mío, Marcos, there are no tracks on the ground!"

Fermin returns to his saddle and hands the lamp back to his friend. In the dim light, Marcos' face has turned to ice white. "Marcos, companion, what's the matter? You look as pale as death."

In Marcos' confusion he retorts only because he believes he is alive.

"I am sick, my friend."

Marcos hastily dismounts and stumbles in the thickness of the mist. He tries to remove himself as far away from Fermin as possible. Fermin waits, he too is in a state of suspended confusion. From the depths of that foreboding mist and thicket of black dreams he hears his friend in convulsion.

"Marcos, Marcos, ¿Qué pasa?"

Marcos' heaves are as dry as the moon itself. He lies close to the bank of a ditch, close to his own vomit of fear. Even the life-giving gurgle of the acequia cannot comfort him. Distraught and weak he manages to scoop up a handful of water to wash the filth from his face.

Moved by the concern for his friend, Fermin leaves his horse to search for Marcos. They almost collide in the dimness of their lamp. Marcos speaks out of necessity.

"Never in my life have I known such helplessness and fear. You know I have faced wild beasts and ridden the meanest horses, and at times, up there, in those Sangre de Cristos, lived in the shadow of death, but never, never in my life have I come so close to something that appears out of nowhere and is so totally incomprehensible."

The echo of Marcos' words pierce the mist, but it does not help conquer the fear that came out of the darkness as unexpectedly as the fog itself.

As if they were alive or their horses could never forget the way home, the trail to the village became the visible path that the stubbornness of the mist had to surrender to its maternal owner, Nambé. It must have been around two in the afternoon when they came to the bend they both knew so well. The shadow of a barren, pre-spring apricot tree threw its silhouette branches around the riders and their horses as if snakes were part of a new mirage.

The pack horse carrying the butchered elk strains as the ascent begins. They know that at its top their adobe houses will be coming into view. The mirage appears wavy in the intensity of the blue backdrop that surrounds the village. The desire to be with their women becomes obsessive.

Fermin turns to Marcos, mumbling words he wishes had concrete reality.

"There it is Marcos, Nambé, and soon my beautiful Florecita."

"Sí, compañero, and mine too!"

As they take the upper road that cuts the village in half, a small child and his dog come close enough to be trampled by the slow movement of Marcos' horse.

"Did you see that Fermin? That child ran in front of us as if we weren't even here."

Fermin only sees the eternal numbness of his soul and is weary of doubt and confusion. He can smell the cheese melting in his wife's kitchen.

Marcos puts persistent doubt out of his mind only to dream that in a few feet the edge of his fields will become reality. He sees himself milking his favorite cow. Then he sees himself dancing a very slow and intoxicating waltz with Juanita. As if his thoughts have congealed into bad dreams, he sees his neighbor, Tomás Archuleta, step in front of him and knock on the door that he was about to open.

The aged Tomás Archuleta has had this task before. In this kind of situation, he can almost anticipate the facial and emotional reactions in people. That is why he is always chosen to announce that death has arrived.

"Buenos días, Don Tomás, how is your wife? Let me fix you a cup of coffee and some biscochitos!"

"No, Juanita, you'd better sit down. Juanita, understand child, we don't know the way the world works."

"No, Don Tomás, don't say it, I'd rather pretend it's not true. Here, let me take your hat. Sit down and have a cup of coffee."

"Juanita, you must know the truth!"

"Don Tomás, . . . please . . . have your coffee first. I already know."

The smell of freshly brewed coffee becomes nauseating to Don Tomás. This type of situation is unusual to him. In most cases people break out in mournful laments and wails reach such a peak of hysteria that he too would accompany them in their tearful agony of loss. But this young girl was somehow caught in a fixed mood of serenity and calm.

"I know because last night I had the sweetest and longest dream I've ever had of Marcos. He embraced me and we danced until the sun came up. I know because after my dream I heard knocking at the door and when I answered there was no one there. I know because I helped ease the torment of fears that always followed him around. I know because he was the son of mountain people.

Up there, even this village seems like lowlands compared to the way he felt for those altitudes."

While Don Tomás finished his coffee neither spoke another word. The silence became so oppressive that Don Tomás was determined to break its hold. As if his bladder was about to burst, he stumbled forward with sincerity.

"Juanita, let me butcher one of my cows for the wake. Please, child, I love you and your husband deeply, it's the least that I can do!"

"Don Tomás, where did they find him?"

"Both Fermin and Marcos were found down a deep crevice. It seems as if they never saw it and rode their horses right into it. They think had been there about a day before they were discovered. I don't know."

Orlando Romero

The Turtle ≡—

≡ With the flamboyant singing of my red rooster and the melodic rhapsody of the wild birds outside my window I woke to the reality that the night before I had slept within a womb of gentle lullabies. In Nambé symphonies were born between the ears of the maize plant.

Within the Gypsy's circle, it was her friend that interpreted interludes. They both had similar dreams, or at least it could be said both suffered from vacant wombs. Both were occasionally struck by the natural pains of wanting to give life. Last night she released herself by playing Chopin.

She placed her worldly fingers on the keyboard and the dying sun outside her window silhouetted her face and the contours of her Roman nose. The slightly blond hair on her face was exaggerated every time the sun's reflection became trapped in its nappy sea. With her back perfectly straight, her mind enjoying the pleasure on my face, she played and filled her tiny chamber with music. She made me realize the elusiveness of love nourished by dreams and poetry.

Then, unexpectedly, she climbed to her mountain bed and from its heights produced a magic flute. Serenely and melodically she took the movement of the golden wheat from my fields and the callouses of my torn hands and whisked me away as if I were a mere handful of dust. She kept pushing her magical, musical love up my veins and I let her. I let her because I loved her music, and she was harmless. She had played for others like me, and she had mastered the ability of communicating from behind her rhythmic mask. She and the Gypsy were intimates, and I dared not touch.

She put her flute down, the piano became a silent row of false teeth and the air in the room smelled of decaying fruit when she began to speak.

"I could love you, Mateo . . . yes I could. You can make me laugh when no one else can. You have enough words and dreams to fill my gray days with warmth and sunshine. Enough love to fill the vacuum of barren wombs, infertile wombs, but, then, Mateo, what would become of me?"

I hear the echo of sterility, fear, loneliness, I've been here before.

This same morning my child eased her little body between my wife and I.

"Daddy, Daddy, did you hear our rooster? It's time to get up!"

I faced my wife and became lost in the length of her eyelashes. Her soft eyelids contoured her enormous, sparkling, sleeping eyes. Both my little girl and my wife's hair flowed into one river of wakeful beauty. I felt I was the most fortunate man in the world. I kept thinking of last night's music, but my rooster's chant was even stronger as my little girl raised the window to memorize his song.

"Daddy, wake Mamá and tell her I want some blue pancakes."

"Blue pancakes? You mean blue cornmeal pancakes!"

"Of course, Daddy! The healthy ones, like you always tell Mamá."

The beautiful little dark beauty jumped from our bed, took her pajamas off, scattered them on the floor and put on her faded

Orlando Romero

miniature blue jeans. Over her head and her tiny flat little chest she put a striped cotton sweater. She walked to the door and pushed the curtain aside. Her little bare feet disturbed only the morning dew that came in through the crack under the door.

"Daddy, Daddy, look, it's still blue outside."

Wanting to cling to my wife's sweet and delicate heat while the blankets of dreams covered and nourished the seed of love, I almost missed her words.

"Little one, why are you dressing so early this morning?"

"I want to see if the turtle we found by the pond yesterday is still there!"

With all the music of family conversation in the air around our bed, my wife's eyes opened and the singing of the birds outside became so intense that all of us, including my sleeping little boy, were caught in the natural and disorderly chorus of birds' voices. The walls seemed to melt and transport our very room out underneath the apricot trees. She blinked her eyes for a split second and the music outside almost died.

When she got up, she took the smell of our earthen bed with her into the kitchen, and, while she prepared the organic blue corn ingredients from our gardens for breakfast, my little dark-haired beauty took me by the hand.

"Come on, Daddy, let's go look for the turtle."

Slowly, as if the time we shared with our loved ones will far outlast the time created by men, we held tightly to each other's hand and ascended the small hill behind our house and eventually to the bank of the pond.

The morning sun reflected the illusion that it was breaking the Sangre de Cristos apart on the pond's green water. In the morning dew everything seemed to be caught in a frozen lethargy. The blades of grass around its watery edges reflected like polished gems. The little clear virginal droplets seemed like tiny crystal balls

foretelling, repeating and capturing sacred memories of other peoples that had stood before the morning dew and had experienced
its same magical effect.

"We have to be careful, my little one. This pond would like to
swallow us up if he could. He'd like to turn us into salamanders or
perhaps little toads or even tadpoles. He lives in there you know, he
is like the wizard in your book."

"Daddy, let's go to the other side. I bet he's hiding in those
willows!"

We traveled the length of the pond along the bank. Even the
fence posts seemed to have their own lives in the morning dew.
They circled our property next to the pond and seemed to be the
royal guards and protectors of the sacred water spirit that the borders of the pond imprisoned and only paroled when it was needed
to quench the thirsty soil of Nambé.

"Look, look, Daddy, there he is!"

As I stepped on a dry twig that seemed to echo around the
pond, the turtle quickly dove into his watery fortress. Then silence.
A little miniature teardrop rolled down her cheek. She opened her
arms and clung to my leg. And with the same force that the sun
uses to rise in Nambé, she broke out into sobs.

"Daddy, oh Daddy, I wanted to touch it and hold it!"

In the magical air of Nambé moistened with the morning
dew, my little girl and I are caught in the memory of ancient tur-
tles. They are the grandchildren of ancient creatures that lived in
this valley when the waters were receding and the great naviga-
tor decided to release all the animals and creatures of the world.
His ship, loaded with the future inhabitants of the world, became
caught between the jagged rocks and among the chamisos of the
high mesas of the valley, so he was obliged to release his cargo.
Slowly, like a sacred pilgrimage, all the creatures aboard the ship
found their homes and began life again. This was the beginning of

Orlando Romero

life and the bones that lie one thousand feet below Nambé are part of the many spirits that make time meaningless here.

"Don't cry, my little one. Let's see what else we can find this morning."

She held tightly to my hand as we searched the bank of the pond hoping to discover some new secrets or hoping to convince the water spirit to give up some of his hidden treasures.

"Daddy, what's this and this one and this one?"

Before long she had a handful. She proudly displayed them to the morning sun and her tears evaporated into the chirping of the morning birds.

"Do you know what you've found? Come on, how about a guess?"

The whole world stopped. The Gypsy's friend played her music, the rooster sang his song, the birds joined in, and the intensity of the blue skies turned into a piece of blue clay we could hold in our hands. My little one and I were going to sculpt our dreams out of blue cornmeal and the blue clay of the skies.

"They look like snails, Daddy!"

Then she paused and pondered the mystery of death, or the abandoning of one's home.

"But where are they, Daddy? Have they died?"

"No, no, my little one! The snails may have died or maybe they shed their house in order to find a better home. You see, some creatures can shed their shells, some can't. Some people go around looking for different truths when the only truth that exists is really within themselves."

"I don't understand, Daddy!"

"Don't worry, some day you will."

Then the little world of the pond was left behind; the turtle had escaped, and the blue pancakes were ready.

On our way back to the house I couldn't help but think of my Grandfather's words just a few days ago. I had been troubled by the helplessness of trying to grasp my poetic ideals and dreams, so I went to seek his counsel. He recited to me a little poem that his Grandfather had recited to him. His words are ever present in my thoughts. He knows that there is a Gypsy in my life.

"Se me aparece
Que eres como la
Tortuga.

Un día
No más la cascara dura
Se mira,
Otro día,
Sale y se asoma
Un rayito pequeño
De tu risa lagrimosa.

Mi coraje es inútil,
Perenne como la Tortuga,
Me entrerrás
Tres
o
Cuatro veces."

Yes, my grandfather and the poem were right. It is accepting the illusiveness of our dreams and ideals where our strength lay. I would love and dance with the Gypsy, but she would never lie next to me. Maybe she was an illusion, like the Payasos and Magicians that traveled throughout these mountains.

Orlando Romero

Payasos and Magicians, 1957

"Mateo, I'm not going to tell you again! You're not going!"
"Please, Mamá, Grandpa said he'd give me a quarter to pay at
the door!"

Because my Mother could not foretell my future or see beyond
the immediacy of today, and because she was a religiously moral
person who had heard all the tales told about the bawdy humor of
the Payasos and the supernatural force of the Magicians that came
to the hall in Nambé, she felt that she was protecting me by not
allowing me to go with my Grandfather to the hall.

"Then, if you won't let me go to the ball with Grandpa, can I go
fishing?"

"Yes, I guess so, if you've done all your work."

I lied. It had all been pre-arranged. My Grandfather and I had
agreed to the fishing story if she failed to let me go with him.

I busied myself with pretending I was digging for earthworms.
As soon as I felt I had convinced myself, as well as my Mother, I
walked to our meeting place. Out of sight and in the arroyo stood
my Grandfather's old and weathered pick-up.

In his ageless voice, he shouted with the excitement of a child going to a fair.

"Hurry, Mateo! We're going to be late!"

He sped up the arroyo in a cloud of loose sand and excitement woven from the loom of his own memory. Reaching the pavement he overlooked the stop sign and lurched the old truck into a painful groan coming from a careless shift into second gear. The shovel he always kept in the back rocked from side to side as the old truck sped down the road destined to deliver its occupants to the source of the commotion that had stirred the village since yesterday. The traveling troupe of Payasos and Magicians that occasionally came to Nambé were here to perform for us once again.

We stood in a short line as my Grandfather fumbled for the coins that would guarantee us a seat.

"Ah, Don Joaquín, how is your mill running?"

"Did you see that, Mateo? He remembered my name. Maybe it was three years ago when we first talked and then only for a few minutes. These wizards, they never forget anything!"

We walked into the depths of the hall. Long handmade benches were all neatly arranged so that the small stage was visible to all of those who came in the afternoon to partake in the mystery of illusion and to have the burden of their toil in the fields lifted and forgotten, even if just for an afternoon. Most of the benches were taken by the male populace; the few women there were the more adventuresome widows and those whose husbands never went anywhere without them. We almost ended up sitting on the last bench, but even then we had a good view of the stage. A few minutes after we sat down, a little old wrinkled woman came in and sat beside us. It seemed as if all the elements of nature and living could be traced on her face. The black shawl surrounding her face made her features even more pronounced. I whispered to my Grandfather.

"Grandpa, who is she?"

He tried to look at her face, but the shawl concealed her soul.

Orlando Romero

"I don't know, Mateo. I don't think she's from around here. Never mind, can't you see they are about to begin?"

For a minute the entire hall became pitch black, but gradually some of the sun's rays penetrated the dark, course material that the Magicians used to cover the small windows of the hall. Unexpectedly, where the stage was, the entire front part of the hall shone with a brightness of white blinding light so severe that both my Grandfather and I, as well as most of the people there, had to turn our faces away from the stage. When we returned our vision to the stage, it seemed as if the intensity of the light had decreased and from the center of two six-foot-high mirrors or reflectors there appeared a beautiful woman with ebony hair and dark sparkling eyes. It was hard to tell if she had a waist or if it melted into and became a part of a red butterfly's body. The edge of her wings were dipped in a pearlescent white. Before we could even blink our eyes, she flew around the hall scattering her essence between the rows of people so that even the smell of clover and the freshness of the alfalfa fields seemed to be only secondary to the smell of this creature from another world.

Then, like the note of a hypnotic mountain flute, a voice called from the back of the hall.

"Veronia, Veronia . . . come here to your creator's arms."

All of us turned around. It was one of the Magicians who was calling the flying creature. With the flutter of her wings making music and recalling in all of us the sense of touch, we seemed to want to reach out and capture the beautiful creature that was slowly transforming into the size of the brightly colored moths that could be found throughout Nambé. The light that was so bright before in its incredible size and force was now disappearing into a distant tiny star. The entire hall became dark again except for the tiny star that was disappearing into the Magician's breast. When the hall was returned to its normal dimness, only I noticed that the old and wrinkled woman who was sitting beside us had disappeared.

"Ladies and Gentlemen of Nambé, let me introduce to you the world renowned Payasos of our troupe! Not the Americano nor the European Payasos of the greatest shows can compare with ours! Ladies and Gentlemen, look with your eyes and ears, and see yourselves in their humor and actions."

The announcer disappeared behind the screens on the stage and another man came out dressed in a black coat with silver buttons and red braids of twisted cloth hanging from the shoulders and clipped on to silver buttons. With the force of our native language, he addressed himself to us.

"Señoras, Señoritas y Caballeros, les presento el arte de illusion y los Payasos que ni dicen mentiras o verdades."

Then he walked to the edge of the little stage.

> "Entre un ramo y una flor
> cantan dos tristes cananos:
> 'Acabandose el amor
> se comienzan los agravios.
> Y es para mayor dolor,'
> escriben los hombres sabios."

Then he disappeared as quickly as he had come out.

For a minute there was no one on stage. In the afternoon sun of Nambé that came in through the small window on the west wall of the hall, the intensity of the wavy heat bathed one lone Payaso on the stage. He was dressed in the fashion of an 18th century northern New Mexico pastor. Yet his face was exaggerated in its painted features. He looked tired and weary, as if he had been away from home for a long time. With his wooden staff he beats on the floor and asks, but hears no reply.

"Woman, woman where are you? It is your man who has come home after many months with the Basques and the sheep!"

He continues to question as he pretends to knock severely on his woman's door.

"I know the hour is late, but it has been many months since I've held you in my arms. I beseech you, woman, open this door!"

The hall gets dark again and a great deal of shuffling on stage heightens my early experiences with the wonder of the people who hide the afternoon sun in order to create illusions.

When the afternoon's light is returned to the stage again, the scene has changed completely. On a makeshift bed there lay above the covers an enormous woman with one of the most beautiful faces I had ever seen. She was fat beyond belief and her lacy negligee, which showed a good portion of her gigantic cow breasts, made all of us close to the earth a little uneasy. She could probably give life to all of us there.

Next to her, in a semi-reclining position, a man twice her size too small, held a bottle of brownish liquid. He had the look of a lover. He stared deeply into her eyes. His face was as beautiful as hers.

After a second of suspended animation, contrived especially for the audience, they were released to act their parts.

"Señorita mía, enjoy yourself! Have another drink."

As she holds out her glass to him, he lightens up with an idea.

"I love you so much that I have to read you this little verse that I found.

> Dicen que lo azul es cielo,
> lo colorado alegria.
> Mi alma vistete de verde,
> que eres la esperanza mía."

Her face lights up like the moon, but the mood is broken as she burps out the strong whiskey. The lover, nonetheless, is excited into picking up a guitar that is nearby. He sings for her and dances around the bed that takes up all the stage. The audience at this point is almost in hysterics because the fat lady has joined the little man and the entire hall seems to shake under her weight. The little man has lost his baggy pants in the commotion and as the fat lady picks him up and holds him in her arms both fall on the bed. The bed breaks and the pillows and mattress burst as goose feathers float down to tickle and cover our faces. It was as if an enormous, white fluffy cloud has settled on us.

Then, as all light on the stage dissolves into darkness, we hear the shepherd speak.

"Woman, I know you're hiding somewhere in this darkness with another man!"

With the same burning light that blinded us before the Magicians, like the director of a play, manipulate the clowns on stage. They decrease the light so what appears before us seems to be unreal. The shepherd is caught in a shimmering spider web and around him dance a group of women dressed as birds, but on their legs they wear tights covered with tiny shimmering mirrors.

"Shepherd, shepherd, in the darkness of your doubts and the solitude of your vocation, you've confused appearances for reality!"

As the hall turns to night again a shot from among the crowd terrifies the people. It sounds like a real gunshot as someone near the stage screams. In the commotion the light is returned to the hall. An overpowering impulse pushes me toward the stage and the slumped body of the Magician we met at the door. Another shot adds to the confusion and the Magician jerks as if the bullet has found its target.

Because youth is foolish in the face of danger, I climb on stage and try to help the fallen Magician rise again. Next to his heart, through the cape that covers his shoulders, there is a jagged tear in the silk-like material. I believed him dead, even though I didn't see blood.

When the heat of life returned to the arm I was holding, I realized he was not mortally wounded. The continuing commotion brought a shout from the audience.

"Make fun of me will you! I'll kill every one of you before the sun sets!"

Before the stranger in the audience had a chance to aim at the stage again, an ebony hand that looked like twice the size of most men's hands grabbed the arm that had brought near destruction. The towering giant had been summoned by the Magician.

To my amazement, as well as everyone else, the Magician stood up as if nothing had occurred and commands the giant.

"Take him outside that I may cure his malady!"

With the continuation of the show, filled with ribald humor and a bit of the burlesque, most everyone there put the previous incident as part of the very real-like illusion for which the Magicians and Payasos were famous.

As the villagers filed out, you could see on their faces that they had been entertained. The reprieve from their fields was short but worthy of memory. In this quiet village it would be the center of conversation for months to come.

As my grandfather and I sat in the truck, he visually scolded me for having been foolish in advancing toward the stage. Everyone would know that he brought me to see the Payasos, but, then, as if he too had a young heart, he smiled at me and I knew everything was going to be alright. He knew everything in life had a purpose. I didn't tell him that the Magician had given me something and that I kept it secure in the small leather bag that held my arrowheads.

Wisdom ≡

≡ "Mateo, Mateo! Spend the night with me. It's natural you spend the night with me!"

She paused and I could see the need in her soul and in her honey hair for someone to comfort and caress her most intimate solitude. I was touched by the echo of her mournful green eyes and the magic of her welcomed words. Her land was beyond my fondest dreams, and I longed to destroy the stagnancies of living in her fertile green womb. Yet, even in the magnetism of her aura, I saw her as one of the Santos I had carved and gave life to. In one agonized moment I was to decide my eternity. So, to avoid my own reply, I suspended myself from her room and covered myself with the earth of Nambé. I gazed at her herbal garden between her breasts and I saw the golden wheat of Nambé sway in the wind when Nambé was young and virginity meant we were in constant touch with our essence. In her garden I found a wild leek with long thin leaves pointing to heaven and to dreams of old women dancing with the spirit of their youths. I took the leek within the rage of my fists and cursed it for not having provided me with the reply and the music I needed to answer the woman who asked me to spend the night with her.

She knew there was no answer. She knew that the force of the morning sun in Nambé would see me in the early morning light feeding my goats and talking to the spirit that lived in my pond. She understood what I said even if I didn't speak a word. She understood as well as the stars above her adobe roof that I, too, was an illusion she had created.

She was going to speak, and I as a fortune teller and reader of the dreams that lay in her long graceful hands, took my fingertips and stopped her words.

"There is no need to speak. The night is but a passing darkness that will be forgotten in the light of the morning sun. A very long time ago, when I was a child, I used to be afraid of death. But now death is not having someone to love. While the wolves and the coyotes howl, I remember being a general liberating all the people who had died of loneliness and isolation. Don't be afraid of the night or of death. Tomorrow I will give life to your wings and together we shall talk to the oldest man I know. My Grandfather says he is about one hundred fifty years old. Everyone in the village knows he is a man of wisdom. They seek his counsel, and in his words the way to life."

On the way home that night I began to remember it had been at least twenty or so years since I had seen him. The most lingering memories of the old sage were when I used to sit by him during Mass. I was just a little boy. He used to cough and that was a signal he was passing me one of his homemade crystal candies. One time I didn't eat the crystal and took it home instead. That night it glowed so brightly that I had to cover it in a soft leather bag I used for my arrowheads. Because everything was in Latin and very mysterious in the old Masses, he would meditate on his beads. His beads were so worn that they seemed to disappear in his gigantic and weathered hands. We would always make the same deal after Mass. If he gave me a ride on his wagon and let me hold the reins, I would always pay him back with a bucket of apricots. My Grandfather used to say he was over a hundred years old then. I believed him to be ageless.

Morning.

I rapped softly on her door. I felt myself a blackbird not knowing my true color or the origin of my home, but assured that soon I would be close to my poetic ideal. I could see through her door, and could feel the warmth between the covers of her dreams. I longed to caress her cheek and awake her with the gentlest of my embraces.

"Come in and have some tea and toast while I dress," she said.

The tea had been made and the smell of the raisin bread reminded me of my Mother's own recipe for homemade bread and the way it used to smell up the entire house with memories of wheat ground in our own mill.

While she dressed, I talked to Ignacio.

"You are indeed a fortunate cat to have such a mistress. I would give you a royal trout dinner if you would let me take your place for one night, and you take mine."

But he just stared at me with his pale eyes. He wouldn't be persuaded even if I could bring him the king mouse that eats only the cheese from the light of orange August moons. He knew his mistress was a widow, even though she had never married. I had a strange feeling that once before Ignacio had been a poet, or a worldwide traveler, an observer of human beings and their dreams. Until the moment we left the warmth of his purring, his eyes followed my every move.

On the way to the old one's house we both sat quietly in our seats and let the magic of the mesas, piñon trees and the ruggedness of the land absorb our wishes and our innermost desires. That's the way it is in this land of paradoxes, enigmas and solitude. In this land, time means nothing and everything. Every second is burdened with joy and sorrow. So it was that I, a mortal, was trying to give life to the wings of a Gypsy who didn't know she was one.

Orlando Romero

We turned off to the right onto the road that would take us into the very soul of my village. Yes, mine, the way my Mother was mine, or the way my Grandfather's words were mine, and the way my water gave life to my maize plants. Yes, mine, because deep inside of me I knew man's dreams were immortal.

The old cottonwoods that lined the small stream on both sides were there as witness, observing days when the stream was a river, high and proud, and now the size of a small creek that everybody called a river even though little children cooled their summer feet by wading across it. Instead of being a daring young man, the river was a gentle grandfather, and our grandchildren will be our second chance at wisdom.

When we got to the church I stopped the car.

"We have to stop here so that you can see the village in the morning light. It's a high point and you can even see some of the roof tops. We have to stop even if it's just for a few minutes so that we can both see why you and I can't be lovers."

When we got back in the car I knew Nambé had already begun to affect her.

"Mateo, we can be lovers, but only in our own ways."

We drove another mile and the magnificence of the Sangre de Cristo Mountains stood before our eyes, silently reminding us that only an act of nature could change their namesake and that was highly improbable because the world would always have a Savoir even though He might remain unknown.

For the first time in almost ten years, I was once again to be in the presence of the old one. He was like these mountains, he made me tremble with excitement and mystery. I never understood why, but that is not important. He was sitting in the morning sun with his calico cat and I wondered how many mornings and star-filled nights, and how many Gypsies he had known. His hair was the color of the snow that stubbornly remained on the peaks, and the darkness of his skin was darker than the adobe wall. The entire light of the moment was filled with a strumming of a gentle lullaby that only his aura could produce. Half awake, half asleep, this gentle warrior of wisdom and truth sat stroking his calico cat as if he was my little boy stroking his own pet cat. As we approached, a chorus of wild birds heightened his presence, and the squirrels and rabbits of the nearby fields came to see who he had spoken to as he signaled us to come closer. They formed a line at the edge of the field and their number almost embarrassed me that we might disturb their St. Francis.

"Forgive me, children, that my eyesight is not what it used to be. Come closer!"

"It is only my friend and I, Don Agustín. I hope we haven't disturbed your morning. Buenos días. ¿Cómo 'manesió?"

He stood with the help of an old stick, and I could tell he was trying to recognize my voice. His calico cat disappeared into an enormous pile of piñon wood that kept his ancient house warm during the winter months. In the gray and weathered dreams of the towering cottonwood trees that surrounded his life, Don Agustín, the old one, still had that dignity of the land that refused to give up its virginity and innocence no matter how many plows had turned over its topsoil. This was evident by observing the physical characteristics of his weathered body: he knew the realities of living, but he stubbornly clung to the force and mystery of living. He had outlived governments politicians and promises, and with every sunrise it was said he still chanted to the earth and God the traditional alabado that he had learned as a child when he was promised to the Penitente Brotherhood. He was full of life and dreams, and his aura was a reflection of the man who was born within the green fertile womb of Nambé.

"Come closer, my children, this sun is so bright, I only see two gems reflecting in the light. Come here, sit with me under the soothing shade of my portal. Can you smell the coffee? It's not good for me but every now and then I indulge myself with little treats. Please sit here by me and have some coffee!"

Orlando Romero

While Don Agustín, the ancient one, poured coffee in his house, and while the morning sun of Nambé caught and trapped the Gypsy's face in the shimmering light that broke through the heavy vines that smothered the porch, I wondered if Don Agustín would be able to see the serpents that had tried to tie up my soul.

He returned with three cups of coffee on a hand-carved tray and the smell of the chamiso wood he occasionally used to spice his kitchen. The smell was so intoxicating that both of us seemed to be carried away into the roots and soul of the hypnotic sage. My Grandfather would always say that the chamiso hediondo, a type of mesquite bush, was always used inside the soles of their moccasins in the winter when they were herding goats. People who had pains deep inside of them used to rub the chamiso hediondo so that it would penetrate into the pores of the skin and its warmth would relieve the aching of the mountains.

He sat down beside us and slowly sipped his coffee without saying a word, all the time looking at the Gypsy's face and slowly and minutely going over my features. Then his face lighted up and he abruptly put his coffee cup down, he had recognized me.

"Mateito, my beautiful Mateito!"

Both of us stood up and embraced, the morning dew from our eyes finding each other's shoulders. The Gypsy sat silently but within the depths and the dungeons of her solitude she knew that these minutes were part of the memories that lay in her forgotten dreams and the doubts she dared question.

"Mateo, today for the first time in over a hundred years, I feel a little old but yet full of joy to see you a grown man and as exciting a child as when I used to hold you in my arms!"

He brushed my hair and slowly eased his calloused hands over the back of my hands. The moment was so intimate and moving that we almost forgot there was a woman with green eyes sitting in the shade of the vines. He turned to face her with the feeling of the moment and extended his hand out to her.

"Tell me, Mateo, who is this lady that captures the morning sun in her hair?"

As their fingertips caressed each other's palms and the colors mixed and melted into each other, I photographed the moment. Her true fertility was once again being caressed.

"Don Agustín, this is my friend who comes from the hills by the bay of San Francisco. She used to live in our village a few years ago, but now she lives in Santa Fe."

He raised his cup to the intense blue of the sky and then lowered it to the level of the green alfalfa fields that surrounded his house. Within that half circle movement the light was divided and scattered as if his cup had been a prism. He surrounded us with shimmering light that seemed to penetrate our very pores. It was as if he had taken a rainbow out of the fathomless blue sky and used the porch to contain it. The rainbow was his way of toasting her and welcoming her to his house. She was so awed that she finally managed to thank him between her disbelief. Then he excitedly left the bench we were all sitting on, excused himself and walked inside his house. He returned with a slice of pie for each of us.

"You'll find wild berries I gather in these mountains, I always put them in the pies. Every time I'm up there, I'm always meeting up with a wild bear and her family. If they don't smell me, I hide in the brush and watch them. Every movement is sort of special, they remind me of the bears the Gypsies had with them when they used to travel these mountains."

He pointed to the canyon where he got the wild fruit as we took in the marvelous taste of the berries and the golden crust that had been prepared with anise, wild spices and delicacies he had found in his fields. After we had finished, a little gray squirrel picked up our crumbs. Don Agustín searched the lines of my face for the questions he knew I kept locked inside of me. He didn't have to search long, few things could be kept from the old people. Once again he stood up and went into his house. Returning, he opened his clenched fist

Orlando Romero

and revealed an old leather pouch, worn from constant clutching and opening. From the pouch he took a smooth green stone, the same piece of jade that the Magician had given me. I had asked him to keep it for me. He stroked it gently and gave it to me.

"This green stone belongs to you the way your friend's eyes are yours. You should have kept it, Mateo. I'm giving it back to you because I can tell you've realized many forms of death and the only death you fear is not having any dreams, or someone to love. As old as I am, Mateo, I've seen dreams in this stone."

He knew why we were there and that is why he knew exactly what to say, yet his wisdom was like the blankets my Grandfather wove, a tapestry that was part of the mystery of being alive and dying.

"Children, look at me. Everything I am is part of my Father and my Grandfather and his Father, so, if you like, let's go and sit under that old cottonwood. It's very cool down there and the singing of the stream is the right place to tell you a story I learned from my Grandfather when I was a bit younger than you are now. If you can listen to the wisdom of the singing stream and the earth it nourishes, then you'll be able to contemplate upon this story that I'm about to tell you."

We didn't say a word. We were his children, children that had doubts but were obedient because our search was for wisdom and peace. We followed him down to the river.

"Before we go down, maybe I should take my violin. Would you like to hear me play it for you? Maybe we can sing a song!"

I was going to answer, but my companion had read my thoughts.

"Please, Don Agustín, play something for us!"

From a beautifully tanned leather bag he took an ancient homemade violin.

"It was my Grandfather's," he said.

We sat under the ageless cottonwood tree, on an enormous protruding root, a root that headed in the direction of life, the stream. He played the bow against the strings and then made some adjustments as he tuned the instrument. Playfully, the mayflies danced on the stream's surface, mating and then depositing their eggs. Every now and then I could see a wild cutthroat break the surface and devour one of the mayfly partners who thought their ballet of love would last forever.

"What shall it be my children, a little song or a little tale. In my old age, all I live for is the promise of new life and the smile and joy on people's faces. You choose!"

My companion and I looked into each other's eyes. The moment was right for learning and loving, it made no difference. He had seen it in our eyes.

"Alright, a little violin first and then maybe a little tale. My mother used to sing this in the early morn while she sewed under the shade of her dreams. She told me once she had learned it from a Spanish Gypsy that used to wander these mountains."

He made his ancient instrument wail a wild lament. In the passion and heat of his voice, all of Nambé could hear his singing.

My companion knew all the languages as he sang in Spanish. There was no need for translation. I could tell she was singing along with him in her language.

> With the vito, vito, vito,
> With the vito, vito, va.
> Don't stare at my face,
> You make me blush.
> Unmarried girls are golden,
> And married women silver.
> Widows are made of copper,
> And old women of tin.
> The bull will not kill me,
> Nor the bullfighter.
> A girl will kill me,
> A girl who has dark eyes.

Orlando Romero

He didn't have to put his violin down. I could tell that she was contemplating her female spirit and what she was to do with it. She smiled at both of us and we knew her essence was being strengthened.

The old one raised the violin to his chin again and began a joyous song. It was an intoxicant. We forgot our earthly condition and our feet took wings. She took my hand and under the magical shade of the cottonwood, heavy with the dreams and sighs of countless lovers, we danced as if the children in our souls were as boundless as the movement of the stars and as endless as the infinity of the universe. We loved each other with the earthly sensuality of the morning rain and the passion of August moons. Yet our love was innocent. We lived in each other's joy and sorrow and our lives were as natural as the cyclic pattern of life and death. The music kept on and on and on. So we twirled and twirled and melted into each other's dreams so that both of us, exhausted and dizzy with the joy of living, collapsed into each other's arms and braced ourselves for the realities of living. We were each other's dreams.

For now all that mattered was the moment. We laughed and held tightly to each other. Her honey hair smothered the sun and the darkness of our doubts was forgotten as we danced to the music of the old one. Tireless playing, endless joy, we couldn't stop! We were caught up in his magic because he knew the kind of lovers that we were. We would love each other even if we never touched. To add to the moment, he paused in his playing and for a twinkling moment in the shimmering light of his aura, he straightened his back, looked up to the sky and said, "I'm ready any time you are!"

Without any music, but with the music of the day, he took our hands as we formed a circle, and together we raised such a cloud of heavenly rhythm that it flowed to the uppermost branches of the cottonwood, inspired the wild birds and they too went out of their minds in song. It was so intense that the moment became as brittle as glass. He knew the urgency and anxiety of life. So, the tempo was gradually eased, and all of us regained the stature and calm of the cottonwood that shaded our movements.

In that calm, he knew we were ready for a story, but he left us for a second as he searched for the sunlight through the foliage of the ancient tree. His gaze was for another world, but his words were for this one.

"Children, children, today I have seen God again! Such comfort to know someone needs you!"

The old Patriarch looked at our faces for the right story to tell us. If he didn't have one, he would weave one for us from the longing in our eyes.

"Let's see, now," he said, as if oblivious to the previous moment. That's the way things are in Nambé. One never explains the last moment.

"Ah, I know the one called The Basil Plant, it's short enough so that we may be able to find our way back to the house without having to wait for the moon to appear."

Intently, we sat by him as if he was the Father we never had. He looked at us for the beginning.

"Once there was a king. And the king met three daughters of a poor man and asked each one in turn, 'You, who water the basil plant, tell me how many leaves it has.' The two older sisters could not answer, but the youngest said, 'You who know how to read and write, tell me how many waves the ocean has.' The king, unable to answer, called the youngest daughter to the palace and gave her two pieces of rock, asking her to cut out a pair of drawers. She agreed to do so, but first she gave the king a piece of rock and asked him to draw thread from it. Unable to comply, he dismissed her, requesting that she bring her father who must be, at the same time, mounted and dismounted combed and uncombed, shod and unshod."

Don Agustín stopped for a moment to check the course of the dying sun. It was almost time. Then he continued.

"The girl then brought her father on a goat, with his feet touching the ground, wearing shoes without soles, only half dressed, and with his hair combed on one side and disheveled on the other. The king was satisfied and told her to request anything that she desired. She asked for roasted snow. The king explained that her request was impossible. The peasant girl then reminded the king that he wanted to marry a girl who would be pregnant and a virgin at the same time, adding that it was equally impossible for a woman to be both pregnant and a virgin!"

Don Agustín stopped for a moment and emphasized that the king was extremely jealous of the peasant girl's wisdom.

"Well," he continued, "the king decided to marry the girl in order to murder her. Suspecting his intentions, the girl procured a life-size wax image of herself and put a piece of syrup-filled gut around the neck of the image. She placed the doll in her bed and then crawled under it. During the night, the king came and stabbed the doll, bursting the gut and splashing himself with syrup, which he thought was blood. The king then said regretfully, 'If dead you are so sweet, what must you have been alive!' Just as he was about to kill himself, the girl comes out from under the bed and the two are reconciled and live happily thereafter!"

I overcame the urge to analyze. It didn't matter whether he was talking about illusions or not. What mattered was that the Gypsy, Don Agustín and I had sung, danced and had tasted life again. He broke the stillness as we prepared for the direction of his home.

"Let us go, children. I feel the light failing and voices calling me from the darkness that is to come!"

We had left him at his door with our warmest embrace, and as the Gypsy took my hand, she clasped it tightly because we both knew that the morning sun would no longer welcome his earthly chant.

That night Don Agustín died in his sleep.

The Funeral ≡−

≡ Next morning, at about six, there was no sun. Instead, the sky was covered with thousands of black crows. Their cawing was so maddening that my Grandfather crossed himself and said, "Dear God, Don Agustín must have died last night!"

The crows, as is the case in Nambé, appear when it's going to rain or when the weather is going to change radically. The signs had been right. It rained the entire day, a terrifying lightning storm. The villagers prayed countless Rosaries that the tempest might subside. Little did they realize that once again the world was being purified. I too had my doubts as the storm released its electrical rage upon the center of our soul. It was as if Nambé was going to be destroyed. Its people, its creatures, all its inhabitants and the entire terrain were to be consumed by the purification ritual that had hidden itself at the farthest edge of the mind.

The laments could be heard through the distance and through the thickness of adobe walls. Children were weeping. There was no comforting the fear of the mysterious force that had been unleashed upon the earth. Even the old ones looked up at the darkness in the sky. Only their timeless patience and faith in God gave them the strength to endure the tossing and turning of voices calling from the darkness of the storm. It would rain the entire day. No one would approach his house. It wasn't just because of the storm. Deep inside of them they knew today he was beyond their claim. Don Agustín would remain invincible even beyond death.

On the following day the darkness had vanished and the earth of Nambé was the color of our skins again. The heavenly moisture had been welcomed by the thirsty gardens, and the wild flowers bloomed and blossomed a joyful alleluia. They had been blessed with golden tears from a weeping tempest. The singing of the cocks announced daybreak. The croaking of the toads and frogs welcomed a completely new morning. With a slight mist evaporating slowly upward, the sun penetrated the veil and turned bronze in its determination to warm the spirit of repurification.

But it wasn't the sun breaking through my adobe window that woke me, it was the tolling of the church bells announcing the flight and movement upward of an ancient truth. Somehow I didn't want to admit to myself that he was gone, but I really couldn't turn back. All roads in the future would lead me to his memory. The tolling and its echo was tying up my insides. My soul questioned whether anyone else could ease the pain deep within me. What would happen to those like me and the Gypsy when all the old ones were gone? Who would counsel us and give us answers written on the petals of wild flowers? He had lighted my way and given me directions. In life, is memory all we have?

My thoughts were broken by my Grandfather's voice. It was heavy with lament. His eyes were watery, like the times when he remembered my Grandmother. Now that I was no longer a child, I kept feeling I had been born at the wrong time. I felt more like his brother than his grandson.

"Mateo, it is not time for thinking, it's time for praying! How else can we go on! If in prayer you find contemplation, then it is in prayer that your doubts will be eased. Remember, Mateo, praying is like thinking. Mateo, we feel the same it's in our blood, but we must be strong and make the preparations that our brother deserves."

So it was that my Grandfather and I sat silently in the same old truck we had been in countless times. But now not a word was spoken as we headed in the direction of the Sangre de Cristos. I fumbled for my Rosary in the depths of my worn blue jean jacket. I prayed silently. *"Ave Maria que estás en los cielos, santificado sea tu nombre, bendita tu eres entre todas las mujeres y bendito es el fruto de tu vientre, Jesús."*

But it didn't help. I could no longer hold back the wall of deep sorrow. My Grandfather's calloused hands produced a blue bandana handkerchief. As I tried to dry my eyes I couldn't help but think of the blue twilights with the many twinkling stars that reflected all the joys and sorrows of our lives. Was it reality that some day I too would be separated from my fields, my wife, my children, my Grandfather, and the Gypsy?

Despite the early morn, the entire village seemed to be there. The women were busy straightening the house. It still smelled like sage. His physical being was sleeping calmly in a suit of new clothes in which his Penitente brothers had dressed him. In the nearby fields, the children were picking wild flowers because they, too, knew his fondness for natural beauty. I looked out his kitchen window and watched their actions. There was no sorrow in their movements. Instead, some sang and hummed the many Spanish children's songs I knew so well. I felt Don Agustín would feel happy to see children singing and picking wild flowers. At that instant I knew that I, too, had the ability to turn sorrow into life and wild flowers. But I was older now, and I had other responsibilities as well.

Everyone there greeted my Grandfather and me. We exchanged greetings. The people agreed to what each individual was to do to complete the preparations. Four or five of the women there said they would be responsible for the preparation of food. The men said they would butcher some of their animals. My Grandfather said he would butcher his cow and I said I would help him. Sacrifice to the living or to the dead? Or food for survival? It didn't matter. We did what we did, we do what we do. The women broke into little groups and decided who was to cook what. My Grandfather and I said that we would stay up with the body, but I wanted to do more. I felt that I had to do more, not from obligation but out of love. If I could play the piano, I would compose a symphony for him. Or, if I were one of my cocks, I would sing him the morning song. So, with the bursting tide that cried in my soul, I decided to carve on his coffin the morning sun. I could carve, and I could sculpt. That would be my gift. I told my Grandfather my idea. Lovingly, he approved. But he added that first the coffin-maker, Don González, would have to approve. He said to go ahead with my idea. He could prepare the cow by himself.

By the time I had designed the carving of the morning sun, and painstakingly drawn its reaching arms with the warmth of its life, it was getting dark. Don Gonzáles had agreed to the design, so I immediately started to carve it on the sides and on the lid of the coffin. I worked feverishly, wanting to finish before midnight. At midnight I was to stay up with the body. In the heat of creation I took time out to smoke a cigarette and breathe the still night air of Nambé. Outside, the moon's shadows were playing with the night. The night and the light of the moon were pregnant with life. Everything was so blushingly visible that I was caught up in the singing of the moon's eye. She had praise for my struggles, praise for the love of the Gypsy, praise for my fields, and praise for the life of Don Agustín. I walked away from the coffin-maker's house and decided to look over the valley bathed in moonbeams. I went away for only ten or fifteen minutes, but it was as if I had gone away for a lifetime. The moon is so magical. I see all of my past life in her rays, yet I am full of the joy that my life is just now beginning, like my stubbornness in living within the innocence of my youth. The moon followed me all the way back to my carving tools. She saw me enter the coffin-maker's house and she saw me work until one in the morning and at that time she provided me the light I needed to get back to Don Agustín's house and the vigil my Grandfather and I are to keep.

I entered his house and first I saw the flickering candles and their shadows playing on the adobe walls. His body was laying on a large table, and two candles lay on each side of the body. My Grandfather was on his knees. So were a handful of people, praying the Rosary. The prayers were in turn being answered in the lamentful manner common to us during an occasion of great sorrow. At four in the morning only my Grandfather and I were left praying. Don Agustín had not talked to us. The vigil had been bathed in peace. It was good, it meant his soul had found its peace. At five-thirty the sun was breaking in gentle harmony with the morning song. The food had been prepared and eaten. The coffin had been finished. The morning dew had kissed the opened earth where his body was to lay. All that was left was the High Mass and the internment. At eight, the procession took place. But because so many people wanted to be in the cortege, it didn't begin until an hour later.

There must have been about a thousand cars, horse drawn wagons, buggies, and people on foot who made up the procession. It began at his house and ended at the church grounds. The two mile distance took two hours, and despite the many friends and people that came from everywhere, the procession was orderly and somberly overwhelming.

The village had never seen such a spectacle. The contrast and the melting and mingling of people's colors were exactly why Don Agustín had lived so long. Poor people, rich people, and those in between; those people who had questions and had been answered in truth; those people who were still searching, and those little people who had picked the wild flowers that covered his coffin and the wagon would never forget this day. Nambé had opened its

Orlando Romero

doors to the world. Even the wild bees refused to leave the scent of freshly cut flowers and their song was as alive as the memory of Don Agustín. His black mare was to pull the wagon. The mare seemed to sense the pride as she held her head up despite the heavy load. In the morning sun she shined like the black pottery of the Pueblo Indians.

As the coffin was taken by the pallbearers, the sun shone down on its carved sides and top. It was the sun that was going to last, and even he knew he was a dying star. But somewhere in the universe it was going to be recorded that I had carved the sun on his temporary wooden home. Somewhere, it was going to be recorded that the Gypsy and I, as well as everyone there, had loved him, walked with him, and had at one time or another been embraced by him. We would always be thinking of him.

"Dies irae, Dies irae" the choir sang in Gregorian chant. And the incense floated past, beyond time, as the Mass of the Dead was once again sung in the traditional form. He had once requested it from the priest because, though he didn't understand the words, its chant was mysterious and beautiful.

Because the village was sparsely populated, the church only held two hundred people. The priest decided to hold the Mass outside. It was better. That's where the old one had spent most of his lifetime. Even in the winters he could be seen sitting in his porch, covered with Indian blankets.

The Mass went on and the ritual was blessed under the August sun and the entire valley could be seen through the sublime heights of the Gregorian chant. The weathered automobiles, as well as the new Mercedes, could be seen melting in the August sun, as if they were caught in the middle of a desert mirage. The fence posts of cedar were turning red and were catching flame.

Communion came, and hundreds of devoted people filed in procession to take from God's own hand the bread of life. Those who weren't Catholic were blessed by the occasion and by God's grace to accept all those people who believed in His mysteries. With every communicant, the chant became more spiritual until the Mass came to a conclusion. Then, the people formed a line that seemed infinite as the pallbearers carried the coffin to the cemetery, the same cemetery that held my Grandmother and my Mother. Within the corner of my eye I caught a fleeting glimpse of the Gypsy. She wore a long gray dress designed in a folkish floral print. She wore no earrings or any sort of jewelry and her face was almost hidden in an earth colored lace mantilla that came all the way down to her waist. In her hands she carried a bundle of orange flowers. It was not I who had died. Why had she brought orange flowers? Again memory was not to be denied.

"Mateo, let's go! Grandpa will be waiting!"

"In a minute Miguel, just another minute!"

But the minute turned into a half hour and then an hour and I floated in movement of the keys. I didn't know it was Mozart's Concerto in B Flat Major. All I knew was that the lady on the stage in the museum's auditorium was wearing an orange organdy dress and her lovely fingers on the keyboard seemed to call out to me. I danced every note with her though she didn't even know I existed. It was as if the music was coming from within her. I couldn't understand the moment. It was so wonderful, and I had never heard anything like this before. The entire orchestra gracefully complimented her every musical assertion, and the auditorium seemed like another world. Only one other moment compared with this, and that moment I held so dearly that I was even afraid to let my mind have it for a minute, but it was like the first time I discovered in the early morning, as I clung to my pillow, my sheets sticky, that I seemed to feel so smooth and comfortable all over my body, and there was a hardness between the sheets that gave me a feeling I had slept with someone, or dreamed with someone, that had caused a portion of that sticky fluid to come from within the depths of me as naturally as eating a bright orange apricot, sweet with the kiss of the first fruit.

Orlando Romero

As the rehearsal continued, and the other musicians joined in, all I could do was to gaze at her hands, the movement of her wrists and the gracefulness of her shoulders as she seemed to encourage her body to become part of the music. I was so excited that when they paused I stood up and clapped and clapped and clapped until my hands hurt. I stopped when I became aware that some of the musicians were beginning to smile, almost laugh. But she came to my rescue as I was about to run out of the auditorium.

"Oh, no, little boy, don't ever be afraid to compliment something that is beautiful. He was a great man who wrote beautiful music. It makes me very happy to see someone so young have so much joy! Tell me, what is your name?"

I told her and I told her that my Grandfather would always bring us to the movies on Saturday afternoon if we finished our work in the flour mill. I told her my brother, Miguel, and I always liked to look at the paintings in the museum when we got out of the movie. Then I told her I thought she was beautiful and ran away. I ran as fast as I could. I got to my Grandfather's forty-eight Pontiac, panting. He was angry with me and told me he kept searching the plaza for me. Miguel looked at me and wondered what had kept me so long.

"I knew it, Brother. I told you Grandfather was going to be angry with you! You're always staying behind. You're always looking for something and you always get into trouble!"

$$=\!\!=\!\!=$$

There, in the multitude, the Gypsy had not seen me running in the echoes of my memories. And as the pallbearers eased the weight upon their arms on the surface of the moist earth that was to cover Don Agustín's physical memory, my eye caught Bernarda's older sister. She had been away, but the gentility of her family remained as strong as ever. That was all that was left of Bernarda. She, too, had been as elusive as quarter moons, and it seemed that this funeral was bringing back all the memories of loved ones that had been claimed by their rightful Mother, the Earth. She had gone away, and the next thing I knew was that she had been in an accident of some kind. The sweetness and innocence of her voice was still as fresh as the ringing of the church bells. When we were in high school we used to call each other up to break the solitude of juvenile summer vacations. Who was to guess that she would die in her innocence. Maybe it was better that way.

As the mourners passed his coffin, they left Rosaries, blessed medals, charms, and freshly cut flowers. Only the Gypsy had brought orange flowers, but it didn't matter, because soon everything was to be swallowed up. The funeral was coming to an end. At the same time, the air was pulsating with life. When it came to my eyes trying to comprehend the scene, it was as if the multitude of faces were beginning to be distorted, not in sadness, but in waves of color, like the changing colors of the aspens in the nearby mountains. The music that accompanied the change came to my ears as the music from an old time harmonica, and the beat of someone keeping time on an old cantina floor.

As they lowered the coffin, everyone there turned in the direction of Don Agustín's black mare. She stood on her hind legs and neighed and clawed the air in the mournful goodbye that touched the deepest and most secret part of everyone's soul. It seemed as if she was going to break the wagon's reins and follow her master's dreams into the moist earth. The people there saw themselves. And in their memory, they saw the slowness of their actions and the naturalness of their dreams when they tried to pretend the past was gone. The Gypsy and I became numb, my children were frozen by the strange neigh, their Mother saw her life with me, and young girls wondered where their flowers were going. But then, as if the magnet had lost its strength, the coffin was gently released and shovelful after shovelful repeated a hundred times. Finally, all that was left was a mound and the flowers that late comers placed on his remains. But God's love was for everyone, and as the people returned to their cars and wagons and horses, or to the trails up the canyons, they left with the strength they needed to face another day of living in the Sangre de Cristos.

The Gypsy turned her face to me and didn't try to hide the waves of tears that washed her cheeks. She had been grateful for the day. She was rediscovering God.

Miscellaneous Joys ═

═ September 2, 1974

My little boy has such dark eyes that they sparkle like two radiantly black opals. Today he called my attention to his toy fire truck. He knows every part of it. The hoses, the ladders, hoods, axes, emergency lights, and the open cab; these are the things that fire his imagination. He sees himself rescuing, helping, and coming to the aid of the distressed. He lives in his world, and when he does nothing else matters. If he is happy, so am I.

Flowers.

Have you ever smelled a long row of mixed four-o'clocks in the chill of a rising autumn? Have you ever walked with the moon in September when the air is invigorating and your wife holds your arm and your children walk up the path to your friend's home and all of Nambé realizes there is change in the air? Have you ever taken a bunch of freshly cut and pungent marigolds that grow wild in your garden, placed them in a vase under your porch and played the guitar as the mountains turn magenta? Have you ever cried to yourself because the joy in your soul erases the sorrow that lies in your breast? Have you ever wished you could waltz under the moon of September and the freshness of the moment is the music that follows falling stars? Have you ever wished you could be the eagles that live in the mountains of Truchas and swoop down the verdant canyons and heal the pains of its inhabitants? Have you ever driven your car up to Vadito and seen an ancient couple sitting, drinking a cup of tea under the protection of their portal as September flowers rejoice in the coolness of the evening? Have you ever found someone's pain and healed it?

Flowers.

Un Bandido ≡—

≡The pungency of the mesquite and the crying of the locust and the weariness of his horse; the aching in his back and the sores on his seat from spending nights in the saddle; the filth of his face from running countless dust-tomb arroyos and the fifteen cartridges he clings to and an old Winchester that has seen more smoke than the fires of hell, are the things he owns. His wounds don't count. None of them had come close to his heart. He rides his horse as if it were an infinite machine. He loves his women as if he was dying in the morning, he eats like a dog, growling and constantly afraid someone will steal his food. He knows guns are always aiming at him and his freedom is as short as the miles he puts on his horse. He has no home, no wife, no father, no mother, only the comfort of the shadows of the mesas where he hides when the light has fallen and the rattlesnakes get lost in the dust of his horse's hooves. Sunrise, sunset, high noon, all the same. He takes what he can, when he can, and he knows no one will come to his funeral.

When he can find a woman in the cantina, he cries in her hair, he dances in her lust, he fights for her, he kills for her, and all along he wishes he could take her with him. It would be someone to talk to, someone to rub his back, someone to ease the wretchedness of his life. He would tell her how it began. How they stole his land, how they murdered his wife, how they killed his father and how they stole his children. How the attorneys and the cattlemen and the sheriff and the judge and the jury conspired to take his ranch. How the jury passed sentence and how during the middle of sentencing the courtroom was burst by a bolt of lightning and how the commotion helped him get away.

He wears a beard now. Every poster in Texas, New Mexico, Arizona and Colorado pictures him clean shaven. But nothing can hide the desperation that is in him. There is no safe place for him.

≡≡

1879 Fort Marcy

My Great Grandmother on my Mother's side busied herself packing his provisions for the trip to Santa Fe. My Great Grandfather was saddling his horse in the corral. When he walked into the earthen cocina, she stopped in her work and asked him for a reason.

"Gilberto, why do you have to go? The sun is not even up yet. Why do you have to go? To see a wretched creature hang? What pleasure could come from it? It will probably haunt you for the rest of your life!"

"You're probably right, but Don García has asked me to go along for company!"

Nambé was a long way from Santa Fe, twenty miles on horseback was nothing to look forward to, but as their horses joined other vaqueros on the trail to see the hanging they realized that Santa Fe was getting closer. When, through the piñon and the chamiso, they saw the fortification of Fort Marcy, they knew their journey was ending. Through the dust and the heat of the day, the multitude that had gathered there seemed part of the deathscape.

The air was heavy, stifling and unnatural, as they tied their horses. Sore and bowlegged, they entered the fortification.

The priest was on the platform praying while the bandit Diego Trujillo was foaming at the mouth. His mind was on the hatred he had for justice, on the ease a bullet took to enter the flesh, and on the smoke that advanced upon his soul. A miserable bounty hunter, a miserable bounty hunter hired by a man in Taos! Shit! A rattlesnake had finally bitten him. That's why he foamed. That's why he hated himself. He had let himself get tired of fighting. He knew the real reason they were here. It wasn't to see him hang, it was to see if he would be spared again. Everyone knew of his escape, he was a legend. Some feared him, some respected him, all were curious to see his luck. He laughed inside himself, "Oh, yea, really lucky!"

The local sheriff removed his hat, took a red bandana from his pants, and wiped the sweat from his forehead. Soon it would be all over. He tried to bury the thought that Diego Trujillo might be innocent. That wasn't his job. He was just the people's servant. If the people wanted him hung, that was their business. Right now all he had to worry about was the thought that somewhere in the crowd Trujillo might have some friend who might try to set him free. He doubted it. This far north the bandido knew no one. He hadn't taken any chances, though. He had deputized two other guns.

As the sun shone through the clearness of the Santa Fe air the burros carrying loads of wood twitched and their tails whisked the flies that were beginning to gather around their behinds. The woodcutters had left them tied as they gathered around the platform. They mixed in with the Indians, the storekeepers, blacksmiths, cowboys, vaqueros, farmers, and a few women who had taken time out for the occasion.

In the crowd of the curious stood my Great Grandfather, wondering what the devil he was doing there. He wanted to get away as some young white woman in the crowd whispered to another that it was a shame that such a handsome man was to be hung. A few feet away from her stood an arrogant cattleman and his cowboys. They too had come up to Santa Fe for the hanging. The cattleman's face betrayed him. He was one of the ranchers who had plotted and schemed Diego Trujillo's death. The madness of power and greed was scarred all over his face. It was the darkness he nourished in his soul that brought him through dusty trails and cactus to Santa Fe. There had been no satisfaction in his plot. The land he took from Diego Trujillo had been settled by a death plague that would eventually turn the land into a haunted desert alive with the ghosts of memories that had been wronged. Only the satisfaction of seeing the last piece of walking reminder hung could bring him the rest he thought he deserved. His wish was as fruitless as the hanging of Diego Trujillo.

The ropes around his wrists were beginning to burn through the flesh. The sheriff whisked away a fly that was buzzing around his nose. The ladies in the crowd fanned themselves. As an unnatural breeze in the middle of a suffocating heat wave swayed the noose over the bandit, the sheriff noticed that its shadow had fallen on the stranger surrounded by his men. The sheriff became uneasy. "It's time," he said. He glanced at his badge. It should have shone in the noonday light, but it seemed to his eyes that it was beginning to tarnish.

He looked at the prisoner, clearing his throat.

"Diego Trujillo, you have been found guilty and the sentence of the court is that you be hung for your crimes. May God have mercy on you!"

Trying to deny his doubts, he asked Diego Trujillo if he would like a blindfold or if he had any last wish. Diego Trujillo said no and instead gave a haunting scream charged with lament.

"Blindfold? *You* will need the blindfold, to forget you've hung an innocent man!"

The crowd became nervous and anxious as his words seemed to be full of premonition.

"Hang the son-of-a-bitch!" yelled one of the cowboys.

At the trail of his words, Santa Fe became enveloped in a sky of grayness, and the smell of the chamiso hediondo burst into the air with the power of an intoxicant. The dogs began to howl, the horses reared and tried to break away from their anchors, and the people gathered there looked with disbelief into each other's eyes. In another second the sun disappeared. Before the sheriff knew what to do, someone had jumped up to the platform and had cut Diego Trujillo's bonds. The same man guessed in the darkness that the man he had hit with his rifle butt had been the sheriff. It was impossible to tell who was who. "Diego, don't say a word, just try to follow me, I'm as lost as you."

Some learned man in the crowd shouted, "Don't panic, it's a solar eclipse, I've read about them!" It was to no avail. The crowd had already panicked, and in the commotion they were worse than cattle in a stampede. But this didn't help make the escape any easier, there were seconds when both men feared they were going in the wrong direction. Not until the darkness began to lift did they realize their direction had been right. Mounting on two horses, they took advantage of the remaining darkness. Gilberto Madrid knew the way home, now, and close to his horse's hooves came Diego Trujillo. They raced their horses without pity, making sure no one had seen their departure. When they reached Tesuque Pueblo, they stopped to water their horses and rest the anxiety that tore at them both. In the clearness and the calm of the aura of surroundings blessed with the people of the maize plant, Diego Trujillo came face to face with the man who had saved his life. Diego Trujillo searched the other's eyes for a reason.

"I thank you, and I will be eternally grateful, but we must say goodbye. If you are discovered with me your life is as worthless as the change in your pocket!"

Gilberto Madrid knew it had been a moment of insanity. But his feelings had never betrayed him yet. "No, I can hide you in the mountains of Nambé, and you will never be discovered."

Orlando Romero

He had been driven by an incomprehensible compulsion. He knew his wife would be upset, but maybe if he explained the circumstances she would understand. His plan was as wild as his previous actions, and as he contrived dreams and ideas to help hide the fugitive his blood raced with excitement. His pulse pounded as if no other sound existed in nature. Diego Trujillo listened with reservation and doubt, but it made no difference. He was too tired to run any further.

As they reached Nambé, they descended down the hill toward the church. The light played on the wild vines that crept a up the cedar post fences and, though every post was tight against each other, the vines forced themselves up to the sunlight. The wild roses that grew along the ditches and the seeding wild asparagus scented the air with a fragrance of shelter and comfort from the heat of an ever present sun. As they rode by a couple of village dogs would be heard barking from within the confines of the cedar fences. From the pond next to Gilberto a Madrid's home came the smell of wet earth, and, as they passed it, the green moss and algae seemed to come up the bank and up their horses' legs. Brightly colored moths welcomed them and surrounded their vision as they entered the patio. It was a strong house, and everything had been made by Gilberto. The chicos and the ristras of red chile peppers added color to the portal. All along the walls there were hand hewn benches. His wife, Remedios, had flower pots and herbs hanging from the beams and the combination of the flowers and the herbs added to the air a sort of medicinal and healing quality. For the first time in months Diego Trujillo felt at ease and let the peace of the surroundings enter his blood. The flickering sunlight of the porch comforted him as he relaxed the weariness in his bones.

Gilberto Madrid knew he musn't waste any time with his wife, Remedios. He would explain everything to her, yet he dreaded the look of rejection that his young wife's face might display. She was young and strong and beautiful. Deeply tanned with long hours spent in her gardens under the everwatchful eyes of the Nambé sun, he couldn't bear the thought that she might not understand him.

"Remedios!" he called from under the cooling shelter of their portal.

"Gilberto, I didn't expect you back so soon!"

She stood on the tip of her toes to reach his face, and gave him the embrace he enjoyed constantly. Her face felt good to him and the smell of her gardens was still in her hair. When she noticed the weary and disheveled stranger sitting under her hanging herbs, she became quiet and reserved. She couldn't help but notice the strength in the stranger's face, and his handsome and quiet dignity despite his outward appearance. At that instant Gilberto knew that what he had done had been right. The doubts in him were eased by the look in his wife's face.

When Diego Trujillo turned to face the embrace, his mind went with the movement of a passing orange butterfly. He remembered his wife's embrace after a day of working his cattle and riding the extent of his properties, checking that everything God had given him was in order. He remembered how sweet and intoxicating it was to lie in clean sheets fragrant with laundering, drying in the summer air of his ranch, and how warm and sensual his lady's embraces were under the softness of their love. Diego's wife also kept herbs and medicinal plants hanging from their portal. She used to rub his chest with them when he would catch cold in the spring rains while watching the birth of his calves. But now all was a memory. That's what mattered. It was like what his father had once told him, "All a man needs in life to keep him strong is one beautiful memory that can see him through the despair of living." Diego Trujillo, now in his thirties and bruised, dejected, hunted like a wild animal, knew the wisdom of his father's words. Here in the aura of Nambé with its inhabitants knowing and realizing the fragility of life and making the most of every moment, Diego Trujillo, el bandido del Sur, had found a niche of healing and medicinal peace.

"Remedios, this gentleman is Diego Trujillo."

She was set back. She couldn't deny it, and her face revealed her reaction. This made the bandit uneasy, and made him once again feel the urge to hide in the nearest arroyo. She too had heard of the bandit's previous escape. News like that spread all over the North. There was no denying it, there was no outright hatred for the Gringo that seemed to be everywhere these days. But, on the other hand, he was never really trusted or a loved. Remedios knew all these things, yet she wished her husband could explain exactly how it was he had brought the bandit home. She had heard her Grandfather tell about days when bandits lived in the hills and robbed, raped and pillaged the villages. She remembered how her aunt once said that things got so bad that the men in the different villages organized after dark and destroyed the curse that the law seemed helpless to overcome. But this man seemed different, or maybe it was because she never knew a bandit before. All of a sudden, fear gripped her. What if the sheriff caught her husband sheltering him? She could not live without the strength of her husband's faith. Everyone in the village knew Gilberto for his faith in God and the charity he practiced among his neighbors. She searched her husband's eyes for truth. Gilberto recognized her gaze.

"Remedios, sit down please, here next to me, and I will tell you what happened in Santa Fe. It was as if God had ordered the darkness!"

She listened with an intense wonder at all that her husband related. When he finished, she realized that her husband's cause a would be her cause. Somehow, God granting, together they would see that Diego Trujillo would no longer have to live like an animal. It became as clear as the air around them that the bandit was not a bandit but someone who had been unmercifully wronged.

She was the one who suggested it.

"Gilberto, why don't we make preparations and take Don Trujillo up to where my father grazes his cattle. En el Rancho Viejo there is a cabin and there no one would ever think of searching for him. Up there he can find plentiful game, and the stream is full of fish and wild turkey abound among the pines."

She, too, had become excited with helping the innocent. It was a primal longing to help and correct. It's the way these people knew life. No real law was needed here; people took care of their own. The law just complicated things. They both remembered that there had never been any problems with the land grants until the abogados, the lawyers, arrived.

That afternoon, before the sun turned the Sangre de Cristos magenta, the Madrids helped Diego Trujillo by preparing packs for the horses and mules, by going to bed early so that they could leave by the early dawn's light, and by the prayers they petitioned God. For the first time in months Diego Trujillo would sleep in complete safety, though he was not aware that the Sheriff could not get volunteers, even if promised double payment, to take up the chase for the wanted man. Even the non-believing realized that there was more to Diego Trujillo than what was written on the wanted posters. Twice in a row was too much for most men, and the Sheriff, all along being suspicious of the man's alleged crimes, was more than glad to see the thing vanish in darkness. He made it known, though not official, that any bounty hunter in his domain even asking questions about the bandit was not welcomed and might suffer the temper of the Sheriff with the unblemished record for being just. He realized he had come close to hanging an innocent man. If the federal marshal asked him any questions, he'd tell him his men has chased the man south of Santa Fe, and that the bandit was now rumored to have escaped into the depths of Mexico. He promised himself that he would never again be swayed from his intuition.

The next morning it was a combination of Remedios' yellow tiger cat and the singing of Gilberto Madrid's cocks that stirred Diego Trujillo from his dreams. He was dreaming what it was to be a free man. He wouldn't tell anyone his dream; he remembered what the

Orlando Romero

old people used to say: The bad dreams, the ones that frightened you, those you would talk about, those that were good, you kept them to yourself so that they would come true. Before Gilberto had time to knock on the door, he was already dressed. Outside it was pitch black, it was a couple of hours before sunrise.

Remedios' voice broke the coolness of the hour. "Come, before the eggs get cold."

The kitchen was reinforced by the smell of brewing coffee. By the light of a candle farol, the trio appeared to be a family. It was like the retablo that hung in the next room. Remedios' Father, a Santero, had painted the Holy Trinity on a small slab of pine. Though their mission was urgent, they were caught and trapped in the fluorescent light of the glow coming from the essence of Nambé. The coffee was sipped slowly, the eggs, slightly sprinkled with red chile, were slowly digested, and the tiger cat by the stove went back to his dreams. After breakfast, Gilberto Madrid and his wife bowed their heads humbly and asked God for directions and thanked Him for their breakfast. Diego Trujillo was caught by the moment, and in his inner longings asked for the same. He would not ask God to return his beautiful wife and his growing children or his Father or the land he had lost, but somewhere in his dreams they were as clear as if nothing had ever disturbed a single blade of grass. And now, with Gilberto Madrid's faith and the power of the magnetic aura of Nambé and its mountains, he felt this would be the place where memory was to be strengthened and the essence of his dreams once again given life. Now he knew God never really abandoned anyone, even though despair was as close as a lover.

By the time they had saddled the horses, packed the food, and made all the necessary preparations, a magical mist was rising. The sunrise was vague, like a poem left incomplete or written by a vagabond whose dreams had never smelled the gentle rain on Nambé's soil. Remedios knew it would probably rain all the way up to the mountain.

"Gilberto, don't forget your rain slicks!"

The three of them, like a slow procession, like the Holy Trinity, hooves on rocks, sage, over fallen piñons, through narrow crevices and dry arroyos; their horses understood their destinies, with the magical mist and the gentle rain, that they were on their way to shelter. When they reached a high hill the village could be seen through the mist. The smell of the damp earth was invigorating. Remedios rejoiced despite the grayness of the day. The chance to ride by her husband's side was rare. Diego Trujillo felt the closeness of the couple and their warmth made him lonesome for the comfort of his dreams. He wondered about the solitude, the loneliness of these foreign mountains and his terrible need to communicate. But, he was free and he realized freedom was only a relative thing, and that a man was only as free as his mind and his soul. No, these mountains, he promised himself, would expand and nourish his consciousness. His soul needed the rest from the plague of turmoil. Yes, he thought to himself, he would endure.

A mile away stood their destination. The horses neighed, they had been there before. They would arrive by high noon. The mist was slowly disappearing and the warmth of the sun made the trio remove their rain slicks. The one-room cabin was now in sight. Diego Trujillo was surprised to see its excellent condition, and it seemed to be a good sixteen by thirty feet. He felt it must have been a recently constructed dwelling because the beams had not yet begun to weather. The mud that held the stones of the fireplace showed no signs of deterioration. It had but one small window, and that was covered with a piece of rawhide. The door faced south and the constant warmth of the sun. This was strong and good protection against the winter that was to come.

While Remedios prepared some flour with salt and pepper, Gilberto and Diego cut tender willows and attached some lines and hooks; in less than ten minutes they walked in the cabin door with freshly cleaned cutthroat trout. While Remedios dropped a pinch of garlic on the breaded trout the men prepared the fire. The coffee brewed and the smoke from the fireplace twirled out the chimney. Diego Trujillo's eyes wandered over every detail of the cabin. It was primitive, but strong and very comfortable. Part of the floor where a shepherd's bed had been built was covered with sheepskins, and he began to wonder how they might feel to his bare feet. There were no chairs or table. He saw no lamp, but remembered that the pack horse had a good supply of homemade candles. He noticed the bed was covered with well-tanned deerskins, and that eased his worry about the night chill at this altitude. His thoughts were broken by Remedios' call to lunch. She heaped two trout apiece on the wooden plates they had brought. The three conspirators slowly ate by the flicker of the fire, and, though it was late August, and down the valleys the summer heat lingered, the altitude with its crisp air was made comfortable by the fireplace.

Diego Trujillo did not come from mountain people, yet he was not afraid when the Madrids spoke of the coming solitude and the vigorous winter. As they said goodbye and promised him they would pray for him, Diego Trujillo's thoughts became trapped by the jagged peaks of the Sangre de Cristos. With a primal necessity he determined that the entire strength of his body and his calculating sensibilities be focused upon learning the secrets of these mountains. He would memorize the feeding habits of the wild game, learn their marks and their routines; he knew his life might depend on his observations. Yes, before winter came, he would familiarize himself with every nearby canyon, bear den, every creek and beaver pond, and the many landmarks that gave directions back to his cabin.

With the passing of magenta evenings and the slow cascading of the aspens, leaves turning gold, Diego Trujillo prepared for the awesomeness of an unknown force. By the middle of October he had dried enough venison to last him through the spring. He had salted and smoked enough fish to give him a substantial change of diet. How grateful he was to his father for teaching him about herbs. He had collected and dried Yerba Buena and Poleo and other herbs so that not only could he be prepared for sickness, but also provide himself with teas for the chill of the winter months. He guarded his empty jars as a man would count his gold coins. Discovering wild bees in a lower canyon, he soon learned how to collect honey and store its richness in the few and precious jars he owned. For the horse the Madrids' had left him, he made a strong shelter of fallen timbers, rocks, and cut and tied bundles of tall grasses. Alfarfon, wild alfalfa, that grew in clumps here and there was also cut and stacked and prepared for the winter. His horse had become more than just another farm animal; now he was the friend he stroked and talked to as the darkening skies of winter approached. He wondered if the pile of chopped wood stacked on the south side of the cabin would sustain him through his wintry isolation. He had prepared as his Father, his Grandfather and his Great-Grandfather had done. All he could do now was place himself in the hands of God.

By the tenth of November the first snowfall had arrived. It was cold and the accumulation was only some four feet. As he cleared a path to the horse's shelter, and looked at the store of dried grasses and weeds, he was feeling the doubts of not having provided enough. No, he had, even if he had to ration, his horse would make it through the winter. Two days later it snowed for three days straight. Darkened skies produced crystalline frozen dreams heaped upon a slumbering earth until the accumulation grew to ten feet. By the middle of December, Diego Trujillo's inner fortitude was being tested. Time passed slowly up here in these mountains, and the extreme temperature made him feel even more isolated. On the days that the sun would appear his soul was in a state of juvenile ecstasy. These days were few up here. He would fight the mounds of snow and the towering blindness of its shimmering whiteness until he, repetitiously, cleared a path to his horse's shelter. He would stroke him and bring him melted snow to drink, making sure that he had his ration of dried feed. He tried to move him about in the crowded shelter, hoping to exercise his legs. It became such an important ritual to him that he recognized it as a tie with a living creature in a domain surrounded by a seeming wasteland of frigid movement. Even in those sun-filled few hours of blinding whiteness, the evening's light seemed a frozen blue which solidified the howls of wandering packs of wolves and coyotes. They too knew this was one of the most bitter winters the Sangre de Cristos had ever experienced.

In the evenings, trying to save his candles, he would allow himself an hour or two of reading. How ironic, he thought to himself. *I used to think that when I became older, and my children and my ranch had grown, I would allow myself the time to read great novels and sensitive works of poetry and journals and diaries of famous people, and now, in the prime of my life, I have the time to read. These words and my dreams and my memories are my only ties with the human heart.* Now he caressed the corners and the middle of an open book as if he were caressing a Gypsy's honey-colored hair. The Madrids had left him but three works: Don Quijote, the Bible and a three-volume work on the military history of Spain. The latter, entitled *Nuevo Colón o sea trato del derecho militar de España,* he read little. If he was in the mood for historical retrospect, he started it first, and was amazed by the exactness of prescribed law. Mostly, he read Don Quijote and reread the chapters which made him laugh out loud. This made him feel warm inside. When he read of Don Quijote's poetic dreams and the illusiveness of his ideals, he felt tearful, but soon realized the sheer enjoyment the written words gave him. When he was in the mood for myths, magic, poetry and the inspired revelation of the people of ancient times, he read the Bible. Both works made him feel closer to God.

November, December, January and February passed with the frozen mountain winds that accumulated snowdrifts higher than his cabin. He read, mended his clothes, fed his horse and longed for the first signs of spring. So far away; even with the passing of February, the snow remained high and isolating. The stream was a frozen virgin whose only sighs were the slow gurgle heard through the hole he had cut through the ice. He was now supplementing his diet with freshly caught trout. Every time he cooked a brace of trout he remembered the Madrids and the warmth of their voices. For nearly five months he had not spoken to anyone but his horse. The restlessness of an awakening earth had entered his blood. He longed to ride his horse, Colorado, down to the lower canyons. He imagined what it would be like to suspend the animation of bursting spring grasses and synthesize their movements into the reality he longed for. Spring was the promise of new life reinforced by his past and what was to come.

March in the valley was not like March in the mountain. The snow had not completely melted, and the few patches of grass struggling against the stubbornness of the winter shell appeared, telling Diego Trujillo that the warmth he longed for was still a good month away. But, yet, he was content to be able to ride his horse, even though care had to be taken as he directed him over trails still covered with ice and snow. He was beginning to feel alive. The stream in the light of a full sun lost its icy chins and its song gave Diego Trujillo confidence that soon his solitude would again know the voices of the Madrids, his friends. From a high peak in the lower canyon he could see the village below. There the grasses colored his vision with the emerald patterns and webs of the longing deep inside him to hear someone's voice again, yet he dared not let himself become visible to anyone. "Not yet," he thought to himself. "The time will come when I shall be forgotten, and I will be able to go as I please!"

He would turn his horse around and give the village his back. He wondered when the Madrids would come up. He didn't have long to wait, for by the end of March the Madrids were riding up

Orlando Romero

the trail past the shaded mountain sides icy with lingering whiteness. They talked of news to give Diego.

"Yes, Remedios, I think he will be glad to know that the authorities think he is dead!"

Remedios' horse arched himself' and steadily moved his way through the wetness of the awakening earth. The air was thin and cold, and the visible exhaled air coming from the horse's nostrils made them aware of the isolation of winter months endured. After the realization of their long journey, winding, rising, falling and clinging to narrow horse paths, Diego Trujillo's cabin became visible. They could see it bathed in full sunlight and Diego Trujillo splitting wood. The scene was virgin as if they had come unexpectedly upon some forgotten dream.

Diego Trujillo caught a reflection within the shimmering sunlight, he was not quite sure if it was real. He thought it was the beads of perspiration from wood splitting that hazed his vision. No, it was real. he dropped his axe and ran with the joy of a young child meeting his father after a hard day in the fields.

"Diego!" cried Gilberto Madrid.

Before either one had a chance to dismount at the bottom of the trail, Diego Trujillo embraced them both, and with his strength lowered them off their saddles. The moment was profound. The thin air had produced a sense of total isolation. It was only the three of them who were alive on this mountain top, and yet the rising sounds of their embraces gave birth to all the other dormant creatures and plants. Mankind's ability to display love and peace had been the ember that thawed the darkness of lingering cold. The scene became a wild rhythm of heat and sensual acknowledgment of life. And because in those days people knew what joy meant, and they respected life the trio wept in joy. Diego's bond with the Madrids now had become eternal. There was kinship flow; like Father, Son, and Holy Ghost.

They reminisced as if they were long lost brothers. They laughed and danced and drank the homemade wine that Gilberto had brought with him. They cooked trout and fried fresh steer meat. The potatoes that Remedios brought with her sizzled in the heat of the fireplace. When the banquet was served and the three prepared to eat, it was Diego who lowered his head first and thanked God. The meal and the words flowed.

Gilberto sipped his wine and washed down the tender steer.

"It must have been lonely, Diego, and surely cold."

"No, lonely never, just terribly lonesome. I read a great deal, thought and cleared my doubts and worries. It's strange, but coming from lower altitudes I should have suffered greatly. But I prepared and made myself strong as one must always do when one is to live alone."

He then became self-conscious when he realized how beautiful Remedios looked and became ashamed when he realized that he longed to touch a woman's gentle skin.

"Gilberto," Remedios said, "tell him!"

Diego became withdrawn. He dreaded his suspicions. If they had bad news, they would not be so joyous, he thought.

"Diego, you're a free man!"

Before he had time to question Gilberto's words, Remedios' voice filled the cabin with its soothing pitch.

"There was a shootout in October, down in Las Cruces. Some bandits were surrounded in an old house at the southern end of that town. According to the news we got last month from a stranger passing our village on his way up to Taos, the officials are certain that you were among those they shot it out with. They say that this time your luck had run out because the only thing that was left of you was the charred body they found in the fire that followed the shooting. Four days ago my Father returned from buying coffee at Santa Fe, and he said that the law has stopped searching for you!"

Diego relaxed his elbows on the table and covered his face with his work-scarred hands. The Madrids knew why the sobs were

Orlando Romero

muffled, and why he stood up and left the cabin. They remained around the table motionlessly.

Diego re-entered the cabin. "Friends, this is indeed a time for celebration!"

Gilberto passed the jug of homemade wine around the table. Encouraged by Gilberto, Remedios drank more than usual. The heat of the fireplace filled the room, the heat of the wine warmed their blood, and the joy of the hour dizzied them into dance and song. Outside, the horses heard the escaping joy. It must have been a timeless three hours that they rejoiced in singing and dancing. The only musical accompaniment came from an endless well of human souls constantly reaching for warmth and peace. As the joy mellowed and was absorbed into the ageless essence of the mountains, the Madrids prepared for the journey down into the fertile valleys.

"Diego, why don't you go down with us? You are free now!"

Diego became pensive at the final mention of freedom. He couldn't tell them how he had become magnetized by the mountains, how someone from the lowlands had become part of the solitude and isolation and peaceful meditation that was the essence of these altitudes. In the first ecstasy associated with the poetry and meaning of the word freedom, Diego was moved to profound heights of sublime joy. Now, with the realization of faces watching instead of trees and the creatures that inhabited his surroundings, he became aware of the fertilizing solitude he was to lose. He became torn between the longing to be caressed and loved once again and the need for peaceful contemplation that the mountains afforded him.

"Thank you. I realize how much you have already done for me, and I will forever be grateful to you both, but I think I need a little more time to adjust to my freedom."

He embraced them and they mounted, and he rode with them as far down the canyons as his newly adopted mountain spirit would allow him. He solemnly returned to his cabin completely surrounded by and enveloped in the sinking sun's color reflecting magenta on the ruggedness of jagged peaks and shadows that pulled him to the comfort and warmth of his cell.

Time, precious and enigmatic, flew from its bounds and respected no one. Summer came to the high meadows and saw Diego Trujillo denying his longing to be close to the feminine counterpart that lay half dormant in his breast. In the summer light he saw his face reflected in the stillness of a mountain pool. He wondered how he would greet a gentle woman. His past saloon life came reeling like an avalanche of hateful memories, longing to be forgotten. But in the same reflection, he saw a new Diego Trujillo. He was at peace, and his aura glowed like a radium timepiece; no, he would not be afraid to be gentle again. He remembered his wife, she was a gentle woman. His tears fell into and mixed with the stream's movement. He knew he could never forget the great loss that had befallen him.

It was in July that Diego Trujillo decided to leave the comfort of his monastic retreat and dare reach for the longing in his soul. Without looking back at the spot where he had found new life and strength, he eased his horse over the jagged trail that would take him down to lower altitudes. He remembered his Mother's large breasts, and how he wished as an adolescent to be able to lay his head and sleep eternally on them. In the noonday sun of July he followed the stream, his horse occasionally stopping to drink. Almost at the edge of the mountain's foothills he stopped to quench his thirst. He was not used to the heat of a seven-thousand-foot elevation. He removed his hat and with his bandana handkerchief drenched his forehead with the coolness of the stream. He saw a large smooth boulder at the bend of the stream and a large pool at its base. He thought it appropriate that, if he was going to be among people, he should bathe his body.

The idea almost became luxurious. He saw himself bathing in the warmer streams of his homeland, and remembered his first awareness of his naked manhood. He disrobed and neatly laid his

Orlando Romero

clothes near the boulder's side. His powerful brown legs and chest were covered with a smooth and even carpet of glistening black hair. He was up to his waist in water and was rounding the base of the boulder that protruded into the water when he noticed a beautiful mare tied to a nearby scrub oak. His first reaction was apprehension, but as he rounded the boulder his conscious mind was totally chained and the vision he saw was rationalized as a dream or the reality he believed to be a vision of his desire and longing.

On the other side of the boulder a woman with long flowing, almond-colored hair and dark nipples sensually pointing up to the sun was up to her waist in the stream's wandering to the sea. He dared not move as not to disturb his dream. He dared not breathe as not to give reality to the longing and aching in his body and soul. Had it not been that a beaver made a splashing dive upstream, the mirage would have never seen him. When she saw him she became alarmed, then thought she too had seen something that was more desire than reality.

Because the movement of a stream is like the movement of life and a cycle that no man shall interrupt, the two came face to face in their nakedness as if they were the first people created. Nothing was hidden from their eyes, and there were no serpents around their tree of life. The sun shone upon them with ease, as if the afternoon had been sculptured for them alone. She did not cover herself, and neither did he. The silence was soon broken by each other's curiosity to know why it was that two total strangers could face each other without speaking until the clumsiness of verbal communication made them aware of their nakedness.

"Could you please turn so that I can leave and dress in privacy." She had not sensed a feeling of danger in his person, but his silence and the gazing of his eyes was so intense that she became uncomfortable. Before she had a chance to dry herself he came up to her and spoke softly with the reassurance that they both needed.

"I'm terribly sorry to have disturbed your bathing, but that large boulder concealed you, and I truly did not see you or your beautiful mare. Had I, well, I'm sure that I would have left you to yourself. You see, I've been away from people. I've been living up there, in a very peaceful place." He pointed to the mountains with their peaks vaguely traced in snow.

She saw the curvature and the poetic anatomy of his movements and was assured that this moment was hers as well as his. She dropped her towel and reached for his golden hands and placed them around her waist. They laid on the sand at the stream's edge as if they had become part of the infinite number of grains that were the mystery of life. They loved with the heat and passion of sea salmon coming home to spawn. Unexplainable as the salmon, two strangers loved each other and were caught in the whirlpool of life; they didn't stop to speak or to doubt or to question, but flowed with the rhythm of the stream and followed it to its end which was the beginning.

$$\Longrightarrow\Longleftarrow$$

The last the Madrids heard of Diego Trujillo was from a letter he sent them from Wyoming telling them that a wandering woman had become his wife and was going to have a baby and that, even though now and then she became restless, she loved him and the ranch they hoped to homestead. They missed Diego, but they realized someday they, too, might have children.

My Aunt ≡

It's good to have relatives! Especially to have those who remember the past. Today will be the past, and, since the future seems uncertain, we derive our strength to face each new day from the lingering warmth of what has gone by. Each one of us lives in his own time. Each one of us lives in his own world. It is the health of our own past and the health of our own world that will determine our future.

My Aunt is a key to the past history of my blood line; a blood line paradoxically composed, yet magnetically and cosmically held together. She remembers not only her world, but the world of my Grandparents on my Mother's side and their parents' world. She is gifted in memory. She can recall as if it were in the present what her parents told about her Grandparents. If we have survived, it is because of this electrically charged intellect that makes memory the most vital part of survival. We are born as a people, we live as a people, and we die as a people. If in our lifetimes we have gone astray and have lost our essence, it is memory that will bind our children to the goodness that our first people understood, and which existed between themselves and the earth of Nambé. It is my Aunt who makes me understand that without first realizing my organic essence and relationship with the earth, I will never reach another plane. If I hallucinate a truth, it is because the seed for truth was planted in my past by my Aunt, maybe by my Grandfather, maybe by my Mother or by the alcoholic tears of my Father who longs to be free but cannot find the road to freedom. All things created must perish, but dreams are not created, even if some say they are created by desire. Desire must need a seed. Man's soul is the earth where the seed can survive. Desire is the future of mankind. Desire is the seed, and the seed is desire. If our desires are bad, we will perish. If our desires are good and life-giving, then humans and their dreams of peace will be eternal.

Sometimes my Aunt comes by in the evenings. She appears at the door as a Ghost would. She knocks three times and is hardly visible. The dog barks, so we know that someone is out there, out there in the darkness. Like all relatives, at first there is mixed emotion. Why should a relative be paying a visit? But because we are one blood that cannot be denied, she comes out of the darkness and with her she always brings some light. Blood, like our past, cannot really live in shadows. Sooner or later, the pig's tail will appear, sometimes not at all; sometimes it is the strength of family ties that gives meaning to existence. Woe the man who has not at least one good family member he can call his friend.

Sometimes, like in all conversations, she provides us with some new village gossip. Usually, however, it remains along the lines of family conditions. But with me and my constant search for meaning, we usually end up talking about things past.

Tonight I told her about a book in which a family had intermarried and had children with tails. She said that in times past people hardly knew other people and marriage of cousins was almost a necessity. I told her of curanderas and doctors of wild weeds I had read about, and she told me of how she had been healed by herbs.

I asked her about Gypsies and Payasos, and she warned me that there were still Gypsies who could magnetize me out of my mind.

She is not yet seventy and she knows more than many learned scholars at the universities. I cannot confide in my Aunt that there is a Gypsy who lives within me. This would worry her as she remembers Gypsies more for their thievery than for their gifts. I am sure my Aunt, though wise in years, could not comprehend my vagabond spirit that longs to ease the pain of those who suffer. My Aunt is good and righteous, but like all of us she suffers from human frailties. Her goodness far outweighs any small defect she may have.

My Aunt's visits have almost become rituals. She is one of the links in a primal chain of recollection and undeniable memory. How different I had seen her in my hallucinatory fevers. Those fevers had been outgrown with the coming of hair on my face and the thickening of my voice, but so powerful had the impressions been that to this day I recall, without the least effort, the strange and delirious visions that were part of those fevers. Most of them came from my fondness for mushrooms.

Constantly spending my youth in the solitary confines of nature's breasts, the Sangre de Cristos, I would cook the fish I caught and the herbs I gathered whenever my hunger required it. My lap was my table; my companions were the rabbits and squirrels that gathered near my fire, and my lover was the elusive face of a mysterious woman I had not yet met.

Mushrooms grew everywhere. There were mushrooms of all colors. Some were tall and some only appeared out of the earth like a giant's bald head, always along the stream or under green mossy sleepy realms. Time stood still for the spores and from the air and the bowels of the earth these delicacies became part of nature's velvet shoulder. Never fearing nature, and hurriedly trying to pacify the hunger that nature placed in my stomach, every time I became lost in her golden arms I would carelessly prepare wild mushrooms to add to the wild trout that I smothered in herbs. Only through time did I become more cautious, adding wisdom to my age.

Yet the delirious visions remain. Sometimes they reappear in the middle of a noisy crowd or between the golden ears of corn or in the magical tapestry of the afterbirth that nourished my growing days. It was part of the amazement at having discovered the keenness of my senses, and those feverish visions became part of the prophetic dreams that followed me around and startled me with the acuteness of their reality.

Walking home, my insides warm and full of nature's own gifts, I realized that a strange dizziness was following me because the weathered gray bark of the cottonwoods was becoming soft and nappy and seemed to have a life of its own. When the pains in my stomach increased, I realized I had been betrayed once again. Nature had placed toxic substances on this earth for the unwise, to teach us that everything created by her had a purpose.

I spend an entire week hallucinating under the shade of an enormous cottonwood. The horror of it was that I could not control the visions that my feverish mind had taken. I would see my first blood riding a black mule with gaily colored ribbons tied to its ears. He was the elder with a long flowing white beard and wild hair that gave him the look of a man who had seen God. Behind him appeared a caravan of wandering people. Men, women and children carried no utensils or other preparations for their journey, nothing but books and the look on their faces showing that they understood the wonders of nature and the earth. The smallest child carried a book and radiated with an aura of humanism and an incomprehensible intellect saturated with peace.

As if in suspended motion or as if I had been caught up with light itself, I grew in a different sort of way. I could see life around me ripening and decaying and then dying and then being born again. But I remained the same; only my soul grew and I could feel it trying to burst from within me. I was beginning to accept the words that my Grandmother spoke to me from her grave when my Grandfather and I took her flowers during All Saints Day. She told me my visions were a gift and not a curse.

My family was accustomed to having me gone for a week at a time, but there were moments under the tree that I longed for the real comfort of someone who was not in my visions. When I began to see my Aunt's face, then my Grandfather's voice and the voices of my village, then I knew I was on my way out of those feverish roads.

I still love mushrooms, but respect those colored in red like the Sangre de Cristo Mountains. It was my Aunt who saw me growing in the light of this village's perpetual sun, who warned me and made me aware of the power in those dormant alchemies. I never told her about my early visionary travels or the sickness that accompanied them. I kept them secret for fear of reprisals for having tampered with the Brujo's chemicals, as she called them. When I was older, she told me that Brujos used them on people they were petitioned to bewitch, and that they wandered through this world not realizing they had lost their senses. She was so afraid of them that she avoided all mushrooms. Every time she appears at the door, she reminds me of those early days when I was beginning to suspect there were many different truths in this world.

The Spider ⚌

⚌ You came with the smell of the damp earth that was about to reach my nostrils, but I couldn't believe it. I thought it was the longing to see you. I hadn't quite gone through half the distance that borders the cemetery—you used to like the name "camposanto" better—when a light and gentle shower came out of the clear blue sky with the softness of the rebirth of moist memories.

It had to be your car. I had memories of every little dent, the place where the tires had worn, the position of the school stickers, and even when you weren't behind the wheel I imagined I saw your eyes searching for me amidst the cold glow of chromium that filled the campus parking lots.

I could see your blond head through the watery spider webs that ran down the rear window of your Volkswagen. In a minute you would call my name. I once told you that no other woman had ever made my name sound like music. You just smiled. You weren't aware that even your voice could produce spells.

But you didn't. You sat there. And then I remembered that this was the same camposanto where once the voices of the dead had paralyzed me. The earth was beginning to change its color as the shower increased and the sparse wild grass that grew around the primitive crosses and their slightly concaved surroundings conveyed through their roots to their sleeping landlords that above them the air was pure and sweet.

I placed the book I was carrying under my sweater and it felt cumbersome next to my rapid movements. The shelter of your car and the warmth of your arms was but an infinite arm's reach.

Serpents and salamanders tried to block my way to your car. Underworld creatures and gods appeared with the toads that covered the path to the portable shelter that you had introduced into my life. Enchantress, Mother Goddess, magnetic feminine wailer of the night, you always appeared to comfort my confusion between the darkness of death and the resurrection of life. Soon you would mention my name. "Mateo, M-a-t-e-o, Ma/te/o, Mateo, die and be reborn in my arms." But you didn't.

You opened the door and we sat, filling your little Volks with the heat of our mouths and clouding the windows with longing that lay in and tore at our very guts.

I didn't say a word as I reached for a cigarette and added to the surrounding air the strength of tobacco and its chariot of death. You looked at me and I saw it in your eyes before you moved your hand to take my cigarette away. You didn't want me to die even though you knew I would never die. Do you remember that petrified summer day when you stopped your Volks to give me a ride up Canyon Road? I used a tired and moth-eaten cliché, telling you that I was going wherever you were going. You just let me out of the car because you knew your inner strength was failing you, or was it that you couldn't carry me any farther knowing that I loved you because you were a woman?

How many questions I read in your eyes that day. You looked older that day, more tired, and I realized that even your hair and the sunlight it usually reflected were now only substance of a cloudy dirty blond veil. But even then, seeing you and a side I knew existed made my feelings for you even stronger.

Now we sit in your little car and with the compliments of the recent shower it smells like you. Even your little house smells like you. It retains you and the walls absorb your smell. I know because when you left it for San Francisco never to return again, I went back to it trying to relive those magical and fleeting moments. The smell of its interior told me that the Gypsy would always live in this house.

When I heard you had returned and that you lived in another city not so distant, I knew that the walls had been right. Your walls, my walls, my womb, your womb, your earth, my earth, they had been right . . . we were part of them.

You are looking at the strange shape under my sweater. You guess it is a book. You ask me what it is and as I uncover it I tell you that it is a book about changing one's skin and you know not how to respond.

The silence has been broken, but it is fragile . . . like our love. It is precarious . . . like my relatives who live up on the high peaks of the Sangre de Cristos. It is birth, death, mind, body and soul and the green eyes of a wandering Gypsy with a dancing bear.

I look at those profound green wells which are your eyes and I can see that my letters and countless poems have brought you great joy and sorrow. I told you once that I was not a poet, that I longed to be able to contain my suffering in stanzas. You smiled at me as if telling me that you understood, understood me. Well, that's what I longed for in love—to be understood—at least, that's what I had always hoped for. But you, you went a step further. You became me. We both knew it. It was as if we had come upon a great secret. Yes, you and I.

Ah! Yes, here we are. You and I sitting in this little car on top of this hill on the highest plateau. We can see my village, Nambé. We can see my past from here and to our right we can see my future,

Orlando Romero

the camposanto. Or is it our future? It's such a profound feeling, just being around you! Can you really see me? Why do I get the feeling or the illusion that you do see me, that you do understand me, or at least that you are willing to want to travel with me. Here, take my hand, we don't need a bag for our clothes.

It's all understood. Your Great Great Grandmother was my Great Great Grandfather's lover. Now, you and I, yes, you and I, have been given the magic to relive their loves, affections, longings. You don't want this, do you? You fight it, but just like the dormant power that lies in your breasts, you begin to realize our love is beyond our power. I thought that you had understood the Old Man we both visited when he embraced me as a long lost relative. I thought you understood it was natural that we flow in the direction of our essence like the salmon of the sea who live to return and die on the stream that gave them birth.

I see you but I don't believe you. In Spanish it's said, "ver es saber," but is it an illusion? Maybe you're an old photograph, or did I once think you were pictured between satin sheets in a 1957 issue of *Look*. Yes, my blond beauty, you've lived longer than you know.

"Mateo, why don't we go out into the rain. I want to feel clean, fresh, alive. I want to smell this earth of yours. I want to feel every drop of rain, every single one. I don't want to miss a single drop!"

And instead of happiness, I am saddened. You're like a crystal cut with so many angles that the light does not know where to go. So, all I do is hold your hand because that's all I'll ever have. For the moment and for the future, it will have to be enough. But then, didn't I once tell you that your hands were an extension of your soul?

In the rain you and I pretend. The rain washes your cheeks, your mouth becomes wet and your hair is soaked in a rain of ancient memories. It is as if the mist of the rain was meant as a camouflage, a mask we both wear—mine woven like a spider's web that the slightest breeze can destroy; yours like an Indian rug so complex that its secrets lie in contemplation. We use our masks to hide our emotions, but it is also our masks, our camouflage, that make us friends.

We can communicate with our eyes, with our hands, with our past memories. Our bond began in the womb; it was as if we had suckled the same breast—as if we had experienced our pasts so that in our futures we would have the comfort of knowing our relationship. But what seeds shall I plant in my reality? Shall I say we were once lovers, once great friends and confidants whose tongues once joined and melted around the primal and ancient tree of life? Shall I say you were just a passing Gypsy? Shall I tell my children and their children's children the same story of the Gypsy with the dancing bear that my Grandfather told me? Shall I tell them to have faith in God because that's all we have in the end? Or shall I not try to unravel and destroy the tapestry of our lives and just let its color and aura amaze and prolong their lives? What shall I do? I'm so lost when I'm with you that the only reassurance that you are real is the intensity of your green eyes!

As we walk past the church, our clothes begin to sag with rain. You don't know that to this very point on this little precious and fragile earth I used to walk every night when I was younger. You don't know that I know every moving, pulsating star that fills the vacuum above us when the sun goes down. You don't know that I used to come up here and cry and wonder where my Father was. You don't know that my Mother is buried over there and that her youth lives within me. You don't know that as a child my best arrowheads came from the dark ashes that sit on top of this hill. You don't know that the ground where this church now stands once knew the soft and natural footsteps of a people now forgotten. You don't know that I need you because you found my pain and healed it. No, you don't know, do you, joyful Gypsy? We can't turn back now. We've come this far and the journey has just begun. We are getting our chance, we can dance, we can laugh, and we can weep. We have read, we have touched, and now only the passing clouds can hide our love. Do you remember when we danced in the high school gym, how excited we were just to know we were going to the prom together? How sure we were of our love! No, I know you grew up in San Francisco, but even then you were looking for me in the crowds. No, I've never been to San Francisco.

"Mateo, look at what the rain has done to the adobe plaster. It makes the church seem as if it were going to melt into the very earth itself. Look at the watery designs, it looks as if someone's arms are claiming it. What a beautiful place you live in, Mateo!"

We run out of the rain and into the cover provided by the church's balcony. You look at me and touch my dripping, melting face with your long and gentle fingers.

"What was it like to grow up around here, Mateo?"

And now you begin to shiver because the chill in the wind and the dampness of my earth reminds you that we are affected by the tides, by the howl of the wild dogs, by the sadness in my eyes, by the laughter in my voice. I want to tell you that things have changed. Change—and the word is caught in my throat, choking me. I want to tell you that my childhood was a gift from God, that the old people were my comfort, that my Mother, too, liked the rain, and that since you laughed with me, my life begins more spiritually each day. But I can't.

The shower persists, every adobe structure in the valley below us seems to be melting. We rush to your car and you reach to the back seat and wrap yourself with a blanket and your face covered in that old flannel blanket reminds me of the Taos Indians that used to bring grain to be ground in my Grandfather's flour mill. Not a hint of your long blond hair exists, only your roundish face and the recent brown color that your sunburned face has acquired from being lost in the immensity of my skies. I touch your dark eyebrows with my fingertips and retrieve a sparkling gem that the sudden cloudburst has left; you wipe the remaining moisture from your face with the blanket and bring the edges of it plunging to

Nambé Year One

your open shirt so that the roundness and firmness of your breasts is slightly exposed and I get the feeling that our wandering has finally ended. How is it that I feel you are my home? You are the tall pines and the wind blowing through the willows where I spent my childhood catching wild trout.

When you picked up the blanket I thought my eye had caught the reflection of a camera lens. I asked you if I could take your picture. You knew my selfishness and I knew yours. You said no. But I persisted and you let me, on the condition that I didn't insist on keeping it. Do you remember how slowly I picked up the machine and looked through its lenses, how slowly I adjusted, focused, framed as if this picture had never been taken? Remember how I asked you to tilt your head so I could capture the little luminosity that the darkened sky could afford us? How I asked you to keep the blanket around your shoulders? How your expression changed when you knew the camera was going to capture something that might startle both of us? It reminded me of my Great-Grandfather who refused to have his picture taken by the wandering photographers of his day because he believed that after a person was buried to have his image remain was bad. Some people believed that a photograph kept part of the soul. I would have your image remain, I would convince you to give me your image. I snapped three times, one after another, deliberately extending myself to you through the magic of those polished lenses. I was on the fourth frame when I noticed a black spider close to your ear on the fold of the blanket. I asked you not to move and for the first time in your life you saw fear on my face. Without putting the camera down, I grabbed the blanket from your shoulders and threw it out the door that I hastily opened. You were so startled. You were taken completely by surprise. You quickly leaned over me and saw the black widow spider we had disturbed.

I learned that whenever I was with you we were surrounded by signs. It was a sign that as soon as I had expelled the paradoxical mystery and symbol that is the black widow spider the sun had broken through. It was a sign that your magnetic attraction was a precarious balance between life and death, a raging, flooding stream that brought destruction as well as fertilization. If anything, you reflected natural life as I understood it. Was it because of the chill, or the anti-climactic release of the dreaded fear that you had for the black widow spider, that you were shivering? What inner truth I seemed to deny kept you from finding comfort in my arms? My thoughts were not alone because you asked me why I always seemed to penetrate your innermost parts and thoughts.

You didn't say a word then, you just reached over and stroked my worn jean jacket with such an intensity that I knew I was going to spend the night with you until the next sunrise would drive me blind. I could read without my eyes, I could tell direction like a compass, by the magnetism of your power. Had I saved your life? Going home was such a long, winding road.

On the way up Canyon Road the wheels of your little car parted the wet mist and fog that partially covered our way home. As we drove up the dirt street where you lived, the music began to come in with the warmth of the glowing sunset on the mountains. Do you hear it, Lovely Lady? It is the faint murmur of a violin and the butterfly wings of dreams submerged, drowned and given life by the warm breeze of life that flow every time your cape stirs the New Mexican air. Yes, maybe this time I'll stay till sunrise.

I can't fall now, I can't trip. I must not lose my balance. It's like the early dreams I used to have. As soon as I reached the top of the stairs, the steps would disappear and I would tumble down to the depths of an endless void, falling, falling, being pulled down like a hallucinating sky-diver whose parachute kept struggling to open but never did. In my dreams I held no cord. I held a worn and hand-smoothed string of beads whose every link I knew by touch, by instinct, by a natural way of knowing their power was my salvation, a salvation as pure and mystical as the bright paper flowers that the old Santos held in their hands. How strange those first dreams were. How rude my awakening, and how comforting the reassurance that I had not fallen at all but that the dream had given me wings, strength, and how easily I had undergone a metamorphosis. Yet, how sharp and real the fear of falling, of stumbling, of tripping. I never quite forgot it.

Now she asks me to take my coat off, to hang it in her closet. To lay my weary and ancient body on her chair. To smell her in her niche, to discover the paintings on her wall, to see what she brews in her kitchen, to run my hands up against her smooth adobe walls. Yes, I've been here before, but I'm not really aware of it. It seems as if every time I'm here there is a new magic about her. How can one person cause the sun to appear? Why do the eagles of Truchas shadow my life and why does the feeling that angels have steered my path follow me around and decide for me what I'm about to do?

She's so much like the ocean. Look at her brewing a cup of tea, so peaceful, yet so terribly immense, vast and totally independent of man. Why is it that I feel the cup of tea will linger in suspended animation and the night will never come? Tonight we will not embrace, I feel it, in her soul a storm is coming. It will take another month, another year, another lifetime, another sleepless night, another night of drinking Spanish wine alone while the walls of my house glow with the light left by another elusive Gypsy. Another spring full of the smells of beginning life, another summer, another fall golden and dying, announcing that life will be born on the rot of the decaying remains, so natural to lose only to be found again. My Grandfather says that nothing in this world is really gone because someone will eventually rediscover what has been lost.

I don't need to see her face to know that she is disturbed, that I disturb her, that I penetrate her imposed solitude. Here I am with her again, the fulfillment of all previous desires and yet she realizes the little comfort I can give her is fleeting. No one season remains in this land.

Orlando Romero

"Mateo, hurry. You're so slow, Mateo. You've been hoeing that garden all day. Your Grandfather would have finished it in two hours!"

She doesn't know that I enjoy turning every little adobe over and over again. It's like taking the husk of a thousand ears of corn, every one glistens in the sun with its own radiance.

"Mateo, how do you expect to milk the goats and still have time to go get the water? You know you have to irrigate tonight!"

"I'm about to finish, Mamá. Don't worry, I'll have enough time to do everything."

Then she comes off the porch and approaches me in that slow and graceful way that she has. She doesn't need to shout anymore, she is a foot away from me.

"Come here, Mateito. God, you make me so proud of you. If only your Father could take pride in his children. Here, sit down with me."

And we walk under the shade of the ancient apricot tree where my Father once played. She takes my calloused hands in hers and despite her labors, a warm softness comes from them and I detect a youthful fire, unfulfilled, resting in her breast. I sense a gentle spark of hope; she still loves my Father.

"See the top of that hill, up there, your Father was going to build us a home. He used to have such dreams. How real they all seemed to be when I was young. Everything changes, Mateo, well, almost everything. Your Grandfather is still kind and concerned. He lets us live in his house. You know something, Mateo? Somehow I feel this place is mine too, those dark brown eggs that you like so much, the goats, the damp smell of this garden. You and I are lucky, Mateo, God gives without us realizing He has given!"

Then she puts her arm around me and embraces and tries to hide the tears. But I know that they are there.

"Don't cry, Mamá, I've got to go milk the goats."

I'm so totally helpless to relieve her burden. As I reach the top of the hill and the goat pen, the smell of their manure refreshes me and gives me new hope. Tomorrow I will buy her a pair of filigree earrings from Mexico. I know she saw them and her eyes glowed when we passed the platero's shop. She once told me my Father had bought her a shawl and a pair of earrings, but that he had given them away in one of his drunken deliriums. She had never forgiven him.

≕≔

"What is it, Mateo, every time you're with me you're somewhere else! Your eyes are never mine, yet they pierce through me."

She moved her right hand toward my face, and with her fingers traced the corners of my mouth.

"Your words, Mateo, sometimes I can understand and they make me laugh, sometimes I feel your pain and they make me cry. I want to hold you, Mateo, and swallow you up with my body and keep you beside me so that I too may learn to fly but I can't. Sometimes I want to forget your words, your eyes, your calloused hands, your brown face, your worn jean jacket, your work boots, the way you always smell of piñon wood, but I can't."

Then she turned her back to me and began to walk away. If this had been an open field, she would have run, she would have climbed a high plateau and then waved at me to come and bring her down into the valleys of my birth.

Orlando Romero

La Viuda ═══

═══ La Viuda slowly came out of her house. Even in these modern times she never let go of her black tapalo. She was still in mourning. Maybe it was due to the Lenten season. Soon mournful dirges and verses would wail like endless moans through the darkness of the coming Holy Week. The procession would be endless. The crowds, the pilgrims, the sincere, the fools, the jesters, the lost, the thankful and the Penitente would choke the roads to the holy shrine. Some came for the sheer courage of the long road, some to take with them a bit of the holy earth that brought miraculous cures. The believers on their knees, the fools caught up in something inexplicable, even they knew after the journey that they had been Blessed.

La Viuda, yes, what an old widow she is. Total remorse, total isolation, total penitence, and total respect and gratitude for the constant love her tired old man had given her until the day he just slowly disappeared and wilted like the chrysanthemums of fall that were caught by an early frost and turned black. Bent by time, alone, she goes up the hill next to her house and feebly breaks and chops apart piñon branches in order to warm the vast loneliness of her house. She has no regrets. Only, if only she could have died with him. But even now his hands seem to help her each day. It's true her sons come every so often and try to comfort her. She's grateful for her children, her relatives; they have not abandoned her.

Black endless nights, these Lenten nights. Death-like chills, some damp, driven down from the Sangre de Cristos, some dry and barren with minute bits of dust that sting like the bitter gall that drips down from the New Mexican Nazarene. Such empty nights, these northern New Mexican nights. I remember how I wept when I heard a young man, a leader, full of hope and dreams, had been destroyed. How lonely these nights when you've seen hope driven from you by the madness of man's darkened soul. Yet, I look out my window, at seven when the sun is dying in March's embrace, and the stream of pilgrims is no less. Restless through the night I stumble to the comfort of my kitchen and the walls of memories that fill my life. I glance out the window, flip an electric current that will illuminate the borders of my fence, and there they are. Some are without lanterns, some with staffs. Strangers to this paradoxical land will be caught up in the echo of aching legs, painful feet, blistered dreams. Others will go by the roads and see the crowds without ever wondering where they could all be going.

La Viuda, yes, La Viuda also looks out her window. She has seen so many things, places, faces, tired pilgrims stopping at her house, trying to quench their thirst. Somehow few stop at her house now. It seems less friendly, and little do they know she longs for conversation. Little do these pilgrims know she, too, is a holy personage. That is why she has taken on the appearance of this land.

How this old widow loved, caressed and enjoyed the warmth of her old man. Even his aches and pains, his congestion, his lethargy, his righteous stubbornness. All that was his was hers. How independent she thought she was when she was a young girl. How golden her hair and her dreams had been. How totally strong she

　　　　　　　　　　　　　　Orlando Romero

used to feel when she was young. How brave and bold she felt when she broke the customs and shocked her young husband by taking a glassful of the old-time whiskey made in this ancient village. How good to feel the sweat run down her tender, pregnant breast as she worked in the fields next to her powerful young man. How delicious the tender young grass of spring felt as she milked the cow and waited under the apricot tree, wanting her husband's return from the fields. How warm her first child, how pleasurable to know of life in her belly. How tragic the grandson lost, a pointless war in a foreign place. How helpless she felt as she hummed the songs her old man loved. Strangely, she felt the same way when she was young and in her freedom she knew the need to have a lover.

Such cruel shadows these Lenten days. Now she knew there could be profound joy without sorrow. Yet sorrow was such a bittersweet memory. Who could guess that this old weathered woman, a shrunken womb of dreams, had worn green ribbons that danced in the breeze of the happy Taos cafes. Who could guess that this old, quiet, sparkling little green spring of water had given joy to wandering travelers who had made her acquaintance. This fragile wisp of breakable bone and wrinkled skin, who would guess she had a soul so full of joy and longing memory that she had to cover herself in black in order to survive?

What other color could be more appropriate than black? The old widow's black. What other color except magenta like the Sangre de Cristos, could reflect the heaviness and unease of the hard days to come? The bones, through suffering and living, had been shaped. They surrounded the chest cavities, they determined the posture and position of the back, and the almost hopeless gaze upwards. Yes, for the widow it was hard and even pointless to find comfort in these days. Hope would only return after death and resurrection.

Only on a bright day in Nambé after the widow had found comfort within herself, and after I could make some sense out of the vast solitude that surrounds the human condition, would Nambé be called by its first song of rebirth. Now I understood why the first Hispanos called these mountains the Sangre de Cristos. Perpetual reminders and mirrors of life, during these desolate and holy days they helped the lost shepherd become aware of the need to shelter his tiny, yet meaningful existence from the winds of spiritual death. I was uneasy. My Grandfather detected what was within me. He knew that his times were almost virginal when compared to the senseless destruction that accompanied my times. He knew my joy was but a stone's pitch from sorrow. He followed me onto the porch.

"Look at them, Mateo! They are like lambs. They will walk twenty, fifty, a hundred miles in search of meaning, though some of them are not even aware of why their pilgrimage."

My Grandfather looks at me. He knows how to talk with me. He hasn't changed, and almost thirty years have gone by since he held me as a babe in his arms. Maybe that's why he thinks of lambs during these Lenten days. Maybe that's why the widow's bent shadow on the weathered adobe appears to be a fetus within the womb.

"You know, Mateo, life has taught me many things, and I know that even for your age you see differently than most men. Mateo, during this very sad week many lambs are being born. You've seen it with your own eyes, Mateo. It's in the lessons of this land, in the school that God and Nature created. The teacher that lives between the mountain streams, this close and faraway father, is good, Mateo!"

Then my Grandfather sat next to me. Two men, bruised and aching from handling the newborn lambs. Two men sat there. In the protective solitude of the porch, haunting memories emanated from the adobe walls that supported our backs. It was the endless ritual of conversation. We both looked ancient, surely as ancient as this land, and surely as patient and willing to take from God and Nature the ways to live our lives. The ritual was as ancient as the promise of a new sunrise and the constant blessing of this land.

Evening birds picked at the newly plowed fields. Sparse patches of grass struggled to be reborn, and the aura of the porch became drenched with the protective a wall of peace that not even Satan could disturb. It was our blood. It was our families, our memories, our valleys, sweat and tears of the newborn lambs and the widow's bent shadow on the Penitential procession of memories that were at times more painful than joyful.

"That's the way it is, Mateo, we don't need money, we need this land, this fragile piece of clay and sand and skies of unlimited stars and dreams. It's the only thing we have for the brief blessing of living from it. Yes, Mateo, I can see your pain. I've seen it from the very first time you met her. I once loved that way, Mateo. I know that it is little comfort to hear it from me, but I, too, loved a wandering Gypsy. Mateo, the truth is I still love her, and I still see her glow in the darkest night."

He laid his ancient hand on my shoulder and looked at me with the most intense gaze I had ever seen.

"Look at me, Mateo, you've been around lambs long enough! There are times when a lamb is rejected by her natural mother. That's the way it is, some die, some we save. It's in Nature that we accept her wisdom. We are not gods, Mateo. With us, as with the lambs, we must struggle to survive until it is our turn, and even then this paradoxical gift is hard to give up. But we do not end, Mateo. Why do you think these people line the roads to the Holy Shrine? Why do you think that poor old widow constantly searches the sky for reasons? Maybe all this is for good memories, for a face that will promise hope, maybe for love. Who knows, Mateo, the key is to a door that leads to another door and then another. Only this crazy invader is determined to cover the world with ugly and cold concrete. But Mateo, we, you and I, have really grown together. We have a choice. Love your Gypsy, love your land, your fields, the streams, your beautiful lady, your graceful and spirited children, the wood you carve, and the dreams you try to weave, and, if after that, Mateo, the ugliness of men's limited imaginations keep you from soaring like your beloved eagles and hawks, then all you can say is that you've lived as we have been taught by the wisdom of your forefathers who came to this land and mixed their blood with the rhythm of the universe."

I looked at his face and I could see that his eyes were mine. It seemed that every day he became more like me and I like him.

"I think you're right, Grandpa! But this damned cold Lenten wind and the elusive, almost hopeless spell that has been cast upon me has me wandering about in a state of deep melancholy. It seems as if a storm is my Mother."

Then he pointed to the apricot tree and spoke gently as if the tree, not yet in bloom but struggling deep inside, was a sign.

"Mateo, that old tree there, it's like the widow. It doesn't give up. Look at its branches, some are growing in the wrong direction. I've pruned it little since it's been there, yet if the cold winds don't destroy the fruit, it has still provided for our families, and with shade for our friends and loves. Sometimes sweet fruit, sometimes shelter from this incessant sun, and for you, your Father, and your children a strong branch that has never complained as endless laughter rang from swinging on it. You're no more and no less than that tree."

As the last remaining bits of sunlight tried to escape with the dying sun a cloud of white doves rose above us and winged in the direction of an enormous cottonwood tree in the neighbor's backyard. My little boy's amazement at this wondrous apparition brought me a sense of contentment and as he settled in my arms I could feel the warm murmur of his little breast. Then I felt I, too, would have no regrets, the emptiness would pass, the loneliness would disappear with the wind, and the Gypsy would sing of me, dream of me, and see me in the same soft light that was a reflection of our lives.

The Last Letter ≡—

July 1975

My Dear Lady,

Last night, the entire night, from sunset to sunrise we laughed in each other's tears, caught up in Nambé's arms, but not in each other's. We couldn't sleep. We were restless. We could not even lay by each other. We were tormented. Only our eyes and our hands knew. The entire night you paused, sighed, and tried. How feebly and tiredly and hopelessly you tried. How determined is your courage to try my love.

It seems as if last night we saw a procession, the living and the dead in Mandalian symmetry. It seems as if the shadow of the Moon's voyeur light tried to separate us, as if seaweed tried to tie our feet, trying to keep us from our destined paths, but you would not allow it. Last night was as if Nambé was an ark, a safe and embracing calm where we could try our doubts, dare to soar and become part of an interlude mixed with enigmatic paradoxes.

This morning, this intense dawn, I saw in its refrain your birth-place. How strange and inexplicable, two people, talking the entire night, laughing, weeping, never tiring, destined to see each other in the morning's light. Were you so afraid of the night that you never took your gaze from my face? How terribly magnetic this love.

It was a night like the first flowers I laid at your doorstep. Do you remember those apple blossoms, delicate and heavy with temptation? I scribbled a few lines to let you know that it was I who was the tempter. How strange those lines seem to me now, more like tiny black ants that form endless lines, ritualistic processions announcing that the clouds will be heavy and pregnant with change.

Was it so long ago, that winter of your solitude, when I, like a sentinel, stumbled through burning snows to discover that you eagerly awaited my company? How deep was your life that I fell into this chasm of continual memory? How long was that winter and that spring and that summer and that autumn that now all time seems to leave only an illusion of vague yet intense moments shared in great joy and sorrow? In this one night we seemed to have existed only for the purpose of making all other seasons bearable.

We must live without each other. It seems we died that same night.

So here I am writing a letter to a dead woman. Or were we expelled from the garden? Are you an old woman who cannot forsake the temptation of peeking into her ancient chest, unfolding a wrinkled white satin dress that needs but the breeze of reality for it to crumble before her very eyes?

Who are you, ancient memory? Are you the Daughter of those early traveling Gypsies and Magicians? Or are you older still, as old as Nambé itself?

Who was your Father and your Mother? Or were you born between two stars that I created? What makes you like the sweet earth I plant and irrigate? What makes your kisses bleed like

Orlando Romero

the Sangre de Cristos? Where does the magnetism of your magic come from? Are you my Father's, Grandfather's, and Great Grandfather's illusion and madness? Are you as lost as I?

To whom shall I address this letter? To the ancient ghosts who live in my house? If the address be false, where shall it be forwarded? To the orange color of my Mother's apricot womb?

If this message, this cry for help, becomes lost, who will discover it if humanity has stopped dreaming?

Dear, Dear Lady, who shall this be addressed to if you are dead? How will the next generation communicate with the earth and its surrounding stars if your green eyes have been eaten by the worms of reality? If the old people are dying too, and with them the wisdom of the ancients, who will show the children the real sun that gives life to Nambé? If this letter is lost . . . no, no, I must stop this raving. I've been touched by the madness of these orange moon lights.

This pen is becoming heavy, bulky. It is my cross. It splinters, it tears into my flesh. How sweet this melancholy. How easily my dreams pass before my eyes. Now, for the first time I am at ease amidst this turmoil of love, indecision, and earthly pain. Yes, let me become part of the madness that this illusional light has cast upon me. I am at peace. I am becoming a part of the apricot tree. I am its branches, leaves, bark, roots, and someday the same blossoms that I gave you will he carried to some other green-eyed woman's doorstep. Then she, too, will doubt, question, and take moonlight walks among these red-brown mesas, gaze at the stars as if the answers she well knows will reflect assurances for her doubts.

See how easily I've denied my death, Gentle Lady? See how easily I've seemed to hide the terror of death? See the madness disguised? You are not here under this apricot tree writing by the dim light of some inner emanations, so how can you see or hear my weeping? I am weary now. Gypsy moths are dying in the attraction and heat of my lamp.

Nambé Year One

How quickly my life has passed, and I've not composed a great symphony, or painted a mural masterpiece reflecting the life of my people, or planted my seeds in your womb. Such empty rooms, such lost echoes in these vacant rooms. How sad the eagles of Truchas. Magnificently they have soared, never realizing all was against them.

Yes, I am weary now, and there are gentle drops of moisture descending as if prayers are revealed and answered. It might turn into a raging storm. The arroyos might swell tonight, the toads might appear from their earthly tombs, I may lay me down in the storm's sweet fragrance and finally be true to my original love, Nambé. And if by the morning's light I am discovered in the dampness and the mud, do not weep for me. You know me now, and you know that this is the way it has to be. It's taken me all these lines to realize the cause of your doubts.

I am like them, yes, just like them, their chant is my chant. And now, I, too, will become only a memory and fulfill my destined embrace with that which gave us our inception.

I cannot bear it, but I must say goodbye . . . until, perhaps, my son or my grandson is afflicted by the same love. . . .

Adiós Querida,
Mateo

Orlando Romero